From Kirkus

"A college student's journey to see his romantic interest sends him on a terrifying, otherworldly detour in this dark fantasy.

"This may be the last summer break for San Diegan Martin Brown, who plans to graduate from college next year and start his career. Having just lost his prospective summer job, he takes friends' advice and sees a woman at a Los Angeles production company. This ultimately puts Martin in front of Chloë Setreal, who works at Alienopolis, a company specializing in fantasy books and games. Martin instantly falls for Chloë, and, it seems, the feeling is mutual. So he's excited when Chloë later calls him for a job interview—mostly for the chance to see her again. Unfortunately, car trouble strands Martin in San Diego in the midst of a severe rainstorm. And that's only the start of his mishaps. Seeking shelter or access to a phone (as his cell rarely has a signal), he finds himself entangled with everything from crazed murderers to vampires and maybe aliens as well. As authorities eye Martin for a serious crime and someone steals his ID, he desperately tries making it to Chloë, preferably alive. Argo excels at pacing, as his story begins leisurely and becomes increasingly frantic and unpredictable. By the novel's latter half, some of these seemingly random events connect. This sparks a mere hint of something much larger unfolding, but the author wisely keeps it simple and doesn't distract from Martin's purpose. While the protagonist is certainly sympathetic, readers learn very little about Chloë other than her attractive physical details... Still, Martin traverses a hellish underworld so startling that reaching Chloë is a goal worth cheering for.

"An entertaining, kinetic supernatural tale with surprises and a genial hero." — Kirkus Reviews

Author Preface for 2021 Edition:

(John Argo is a pseudonym of John T. Cullen)

In 2016, on a whim, I set out to write the wildest and craziest story imaginable, all in the spirit of extreme fun. I am confident that I succeeded in my goal.

The title, YANAPOP, is a tongue-in-cheek acronym for 'Young Adult, New Adult, and Participating Older Persons.' It was a spur-of-the-moment spoof on publishing tropes…while also signaling that the story is indeed a youthful romance and adventure story besides being a wild send-up of several genres in a blender that are meant for all ages to enjoy.

Some of the many influences for this story include:

Movies like From Dusk Till Dawn (1996, Quentin Tarantino)

And After Hours (1985, Martin Scorsese)

And Groundhog Day (1993, Harold Ramis)…

The novel The Crying of Lot 49 by Thomas Pynchon;

Surrealist fiction by Jorge Luis Borges and others;

Those are just a quick few picks from a long list of courageous, original, iconoclastic adventure stories. I should add that I was fully conscious of the wild adventures in classics like The Epic of Gilgamesh, Homer's Odyssey, and Virgil's Aeneid to name a few classics. That's all I can think to say just now as I go to press. More info on my webplex of thematically linked author/publisher websites, whose anchor site is http://www.johntcullen.com.

Thank you, and Happy Reading!

JTC

San Diego, California USA

January 2021

Made a few minor tweaks in October 2024; same edition.

YANAPOP

Run For Your Life,
A Love Story

By

John Argo

Clocktower Books
San Diego, California USA

Clocktower Books
Exciting Reading for Avid Readers—On the Web Since 1996
P. O. Box 600973
Grantville Station 92160
San Diego, California 92160-0973

John T. Cullen (Author & Publisher) writing as John Argo
E-Mail Contact:editorial@clocktowerbooks.com

Look for other exciting fiction and nonfiction at the website of
Clocktower Books: www.clocktowerbooks.com. For more
information, see the back of this book.

Contents

Contents

Chapter 1. Pacific Beach

This is the true story of how Martin Brown met the girl of his dreams, and how his epic journey to reach her (actually just two hours away as the seagull flies from San Diego to Los Angeles) turned into a lengthy nightmare of epic proportions involving zombies, aliens, carnivores, circus clowns, neo-Nazis, cult members, and other somewhat unusual persons.

Nothing in SoCal is what it seems to be—especially the truth, once we look under the cover(*up*)s and understand how our world really works.

Chloë Setreal, the goddess in question, waited patiently—but even her patience wore thin. Think of Penelope in the Odyssey, waiting for her beloved and heroic Ulysses, returning from distant wars, to overcome monsters and demons and the wine dark sea and find home with her at last. This, however, is not a retread of that story. The things that happened to Martin en route to the City of Angels would overwhelm lesser persons, but Martin and Chloë rose above the sea foam to win us.

Martin was offered hope that he might have both the goddess and the job of his dreams—as a creative, imaginative young consultant at Alienopolis, Inc. in the big city, with connections all over the globe and all sorts of exciting people and places. As the old Chinese proverb goes, the longest journey begins with a single step.

Martin later told an alien taxi driver that he would die to reach this woman in Los Angeles, if only to ask her why she had two little dots over the last letter in her name.

For Martin, that first step in the journey began with his sipping a craft beer at a scenic little bar overlooking blue sky and beach sand in Pacific Beach, a neighborhood of San Diego.

He was at that moment we all dread—first day home from college, nothing to do, no hope, just the past and a bleak future, with almost no here and now except eventually, at day's end, going home to mom and dad's house to watch reruns, feed the cat, and argue with his sister.

Argh.

"What are you going to do this summer?" asked Joe Logan, the only surfer at the rail inside the bar.

The question hung in the gloomy air like stale onion rings at the Surf & Suds Tap in Pacific Beach. You know the place: sort of a crab shack that always has at least one surfboard leaning against its weather beaten wood-shingle wall. Its faded gray-green door faces the sea from across a sand-strewn sidewalk and several hundred feet of dunes overgrown with air weed. Airweed is like seaweed, only airweed is on dry land instead of waving in the murky wet deeps. Airweed (whatever it is called by smart people at the U up the coast) is dry as paper, dark green, and tattered looking as it clings to life amid unforgiving sand and gravel. Everything smells of salt water, sea air, and broiling onions (burgers and cheese optional, fries mandatory).

It is always dark and cozy inside the Surf & Suds Tap. Sometimes young people when hungry call it Turf & Spuds, or Duds & Studs on a bad date night, at other times Harf & Barf around one in the morning after a long evening of too much imbibing.

Five old high school buddies were back in town for the summer with only one year in college left to go, and one major question hanging in the air: What are you going to do when you grow up?

"I dunno," Martin Brown said while picking paper off the label on his beer bottle. "Live at home."

"Sounds like a death sentence," Paul Lo the math major said.

"Geez, Marty, I'm grieving," said Rob Castillo, the pre-med student.

"Just about," Martin admitted. "Although it can always be worse. I could be taped to the ceiling in my baby sister's bedroom while she is away at nursing school."

"In a very scary dream," said Paul.

"You didn't snag a summer job?" Harry Markowitz asked. He

was the accounting and business major.

"I almost had one," Martin said, raising a hand with thumb and index finger a half inch apart. "This close."

"Doing what?" asked Joe—phys ed major, surfer, and all-around athlete.

Martin felt strangely light-headed. "I was going to shovel shit at a tree nursery in La Mesa, but they went out of business last week."

Rob guffawed. "After three years of college? Maybe they misunderstood and thought you said tree years."

"Counting rings on trees," added Joe.

Martin shrugged. "I'm working on the Great American Novel, a work in progress. Meanwhile, I'm studying film and lit, and I'm starting to think I've been had. Like there are no jobs for people who study that stuff."

"You can always switch to Accounting," said Harry Markowitz.

At twenty-one years of age, the four guys at the bar were finally able to have a beer legally, and the reality of impending reality was starting to set in, like the tide seeping inexorably up the beach and turning the sand dark.

Martin with his poetic ear and filmogenic eye saw it most clearly, like a wall of black clouds (the famous San Diego marine layer) moving in—a weeping, ash-colored bath of cold tears.

They were just yakking, dressed for the beach and still strung out from finals. They had gone to schools together in a track stretching almost from kindergarten through grammar through middle through high school. They'd split up to attend various colleges, and got back together each summer. Something about this summer had a finality to it. Unless he went to graduate school after next year, there would be no more summers off from school. Apparently, people later in life worked all year with like a week or two off if they were lucky. That and a whole lot of other startling eventualities floated before Martin's inner eye, his soul, as he tried to imagine what it would be like stuck at a desk like his dad, who owned an auto repair warehouse. Then there was Mom, who worked as a nurse and gave people injections in their buttocks when they came down with weird diseases. Actually, they were well-traveled as a family, including Martin's younger sister Nancy. Dad's business sometimes took him to Mexico, Europe, Japan, or Canada, and it made for a wonderful family junket at least once every summer.

"I am studying film and literature because there has to be

something more in life," Martin said to nobody in particular.

At that moment, the other three guys whooped for some reason.

Into the bar walked two young women who'd gone to school with the guys since Pleistocene times.

Martin brightened. "Hey, Alicia."

The dark-haired, dark-skinned girl with a poofy Afro pressed close. She and Carol, a blonde, had been among those girls in high school who had been both cute and brainy. Not beautiful, not cheerleaders, not mean or whatever, but cute, like the girl next door, and smart. You could do homework with Alicia or Carol—poetry with Carol, math with Alicia—and be as impressed with their smarts as their looks.

Paul was tall and dark, not sure about handsome but pleasant enough; Joe was blond and muscular; Rob was a handsome Latino— a compact but strong college wrestler; and Harry was, well, hairy (arms, legs, neck, even the backs of his hands). Martin was medium everything, with short caramel hair combed to one side, large expressive greenish-brown eyes under long lashes, and pleasant enough features. The guys wore shorts or jeans, variously sloganed T-shirts, and flips or sandals.

The girls today wore dresses, light makeup, and sensible shoes. "We started working at {*Utterly Boring Company*} in Mission Valley," Alicia announced as they walked in with purse straps over shoulders. Carol Monegan was the quieter, with large blue eyes scouting about as she followed behind vivacious Alicia Washington—flashier darker eyes, redder lipstick, skin the color of dark coffee; she liked to say sugar, no cream if you like it dark and sweet.

They all got along great, and had done so since childhood in the Mission Gorge area east of Mission Valley, around Lake Murray and the (smallish) Fortuna Mountains. Not to mention hiking and rock climbing in Mission Trails Park, picnics near the San Diego River, and various student clubs at Patrick Henry High.

So bottom line, it was a family get together, like siblings. Their families all knew each other, along with other people in the tightly knit communities like Allied Gardens, Grantville, Lake Murray, and San Carlos. For Martin, it was a mixed blessing. On the one hand, he felt at home; he'd traveled around the world with his parents, and studied German over the years, and could get along haltingly in broken Spanish, simply because he lived a few miles from Mexico and had plenty of Hispanic friends. On the other hand, he was beginning to feel an urgency bordering on desperation—to break free, to make his own life, to stop living in that same old room at home where in a corner still stood the diaper changing table used for him and Nancy as infants.

Alicia sat across from him once they all decided to take a booth and order two large pizzas with the works, in addition to pitchers of beer.

"How have you been?" she asked. Despite the noise, they were able to have a cozy conversation by leaning their foreheads close together.

"Home," Martin said, as if that explained everything.

Alicia laughed. "I know. UCLA or maybe Venice Beach would be great this summer, but my parents have had a rough time with my uncle being sick—that's dad's brother—and so I'm home to help out. Carol found us these two jobs as insurance clerks."

Martin made a face. "Do they need anyone to mow lawns and rake leaves?"

"Martin!" Alicia was always upbeat. Except when she was being downbeat. "Martin, have you put in your applications and gone knocking on doors like a good boy?"

He shook his head. "I had a good outdoorsy job lined up at a tree farm."

"You need a real job."

"I know. So that would have been a real job, except they went belly-up last week. I have about eight weeks before I have to go back to Berkeley, so that doesn't leave many summer career options." Martin had been an Advanced Placement (AP) student, like Alicia and Carol, and had gained a choice admission to the University of California at Berkeley, while Alicia had gone to UC San Diego and Carol to UCLA (a place of astounding networks and connections, as Martin was about to learn).

"Oh geez," Alicia said. "You're not going to sit home and mope, I hope."

"That rhymes."

"You are a poet, and we all know it."

"Not to blow it."

"No, I'm sure you will find something to do and make a little money."

"I was even thinking about going back to Berkeley or San

Francisco for a few weeks," he said half-heartedly. "I could get an early jump on my last year."

"And do what?"

"Research. I have two senior thesis papers to do for graduation."

"Yeah," she said with a grin, sipping at her root beer as the pizzas were delivered on tall, silvery stands. "Wow that looks good," she interrupted her stream of conversation with a glance at the peperoni. "But that's fall or spring, Marty. This is summer. Maybe you can go surfing."

"I don't know how to surf. I am also working on a novel."

"Honey, you've been working on that novel ever since I knew you."

"You're feeling sorry for me."

"No, dodo. I love you as a friend."

"It may not be the Great American Novel," he said, "but it can be a Fairly Decent American Novel."

"You have to have faith in yourself," she said.

They ate. Pizza was good. Martin felt as much contented as he remained disquieted.

"What's the matter?" Carol said, aiming those huge, sympathetic blue eyes at him from across the table, with Paul Lo's visage between herself and Alicia. Paul was occupied in a conversation about hot cars with Joe Logan to Martin's left, and Carol had to shoot underneath to reach Martin.

"He is going to stay home all summer and be miserable," Alicia told Carol.

"Oh no," Carol exclaimed.

"Oh yes," Alicia said.

"No, no, ixnay," Martin said. "What do you take me for? I'll see about driving for Uber or a taxi company or something. I could drive a shuttle at the Hotel del Coronado."

"That's the spirit," Alicia said. "Then you can relate your adventures in your novel."

"I have an idea," said Caro—and the second step in this journey began.

After pizza and beer, the friends were ready to split up and go their various ways for the day. Paul and Joe were going to see flicks with chicks. Rob was going to read books to kids as a literacy volunteer at a branch library. Harry was going to meet some other Patrick Henry guys to see a local rock band off Prospect Street in La Jolla Village.

Alicia and Carol were going to meet their respective dates—summer boyfriends, Alicia called these young men. You got to know about a thousand young people growing up in this area and going to Patrick Henry. Of those, maybe a dozen or so would remain close friends for life, like at the Suds & Floods today. The world being hooked up in a network of who knows who, each close friend was close friends with one or two dozen people—so it was a village or a small town in a big city, typical of many San Diego neighborhoods.

Martin stood for a few minutes in the parking lot with Alicia and Carol before he drove home and the two women went off together to pick up Carol's car in Mission Valley and drive to their separate homes. They were each spending the summer at home with their parents.

"Where are you going to go?" Alicia asked. "You have a girlfriend?

Carol seconded, "Here or in Berkeley?"

Martin cringed a bit. "Yeah, well, that's a long story. I was dating a girl up at Berkeley, but we split up." It was an uncomfortable topic, not exactly painful. The split had been coming for a while, after he and she had dated for most of the school year. In the end, or at the end of spring term, they'd known in their hearts that they must move on. To what, neither had a clue, but the chemistry wasn't there, so they must move on to some vague nada in hope of being home when they next interesting opposite-gender candidate came knocking.

"Did you dump her?" Carol teased, and Alicia added, "Or did

she dump you, Marty?"

"It was about fifty-fifty," Martin said. "I'm cool with just hanging out, chilling, and seeing what the summer may bring. If I even stay here."

"I have an idea," Carol said for the second time.

"Oh no," Alicia said, feigning alarm.

Oh no, Martin thought. *She wants me to meet some girlfriend who can't get a date. What do I do now?*

Carol explained, "I know a girl who works at a major production company in Los Angeles. Her name is Maritza Dusenberg. I could hook you up with her—see who or what she knows."

"I know another girl," Alicia said. "Her name is Chloë Setreal, at a global firm called Alienopolis."

Martin rolled his eyes, not really caring yet.

Carol asked: "What's Alienopolis?"

Alicia explained: "Young Adult, New Adult, Participating Older Persons."

Carol added: "Games, movies, novels, music—you name it."

"So it's some huge octopus," Martin noted. "Huh." Like he cared.

"Well, anyway," Carol said, "there is going to be some sort of cattle call, resume festival, whatever you call it, along LA Wilshire Boulevard, I think. I could give Maritza Dusenberg a call if you want to drive up there and see what kind of jobs are available."

"You could be a famous movie director in a few years," Alicia said—ever so gently but acidly.

Martin almost said no. How competitive would such a thing be? He pictured a vast hall or convention center, filled with tables and thousands of babbling, desperate college seniors waving soggy résumés in sweaty palms and hoping to become the next screenplay or novelization writer, and with luck maybe settle for secretary or kitchenette cleaner.

"What have you got to lose?" Carol said.

"You were going to spend the summer working in a tree nursery," Alicia said.

They stood in the windy parking lot outside Scarf & Barf, while seagulls wheeled—screeching urgently—around their heads over parked cars. The birds were on a kill-or-be-killed survival mission. Each had to be the first to grab a discarded fry or a shred of hot dog skin if they wanted to live to see tomorrow. This was the nature of life in the cosmos. Be there or be square. Sail or fail. Fly or cry. With prodding from Alicia and (subconsciously) from the gulls, Martin agreed to give it a shot. If nothing else, he could spend a day or two in LA, maybe see art at the Getty or prehistoric bones at the La Brea tar pits, or any number of other interesting sights. Maybe meet some interesting new woman—you never knew. Now what about this Maritza that Carol knew from somewhere long ago?

Chapter 2. Maritza Dusenberg

Maritza Dusenberg was, of course, nothing like her name would lead a reasonable person to expect. Martin flew in on a commuter prop, landing at LAX. He took an Uber to a tall Art Deco building just off Wilshire Boulevard near Century City, home of some famous movie studios.

Even with Carol's prep job, it was hard to imagine a Maritza Dusenberg until you met one. Which made life interesting. How boring otherwise.

Maritza was a smallish, caramel-skinned, attractive Brazilian woman in her mid-20s, whose grandfather had been the son of Jewish refugees from Nazi Germany. He'd settled in Sao Paolo during World War II, married a mixed-race woman who had inherited a fortune from her parents' alpaca farm and other business ventures on the edge of the rain forest, and begat children among whom was Maritza's dad. This was the story Carol gave Martin before he left San Diego, to prep him. Maritza's dad had married a woman official at the U.S. Consulate. They'd moved with her to California when the kids were small, and started a multi-million dollar chain of pharmacies. Evidently, they were a family of go-getters in that way, and Maritza was of that same DNA. After finishing her B.A. in Economics at USC, she'd met someone in the film industry. Maritza was a great networker, according to Carol—and, not to sweat the small stuff, in a lesbian relationship with a blonde Norwegian Olympic ski champion, so that made things simple.

"So nice to meet you," said Maritza in her air conditioned glass corner office on the upsky-whatsit floor of the Whosie-wildshit Building off Wilshire. "Did you have a nice trip?"

"I flew in," Martin said absently. "I've made the drive so many times."

"Oh I know," Maritza said familiarly while shuffling papers on the desk. She was ever a trim, sharp blur of motion, wearing a short, black-and-white pattern dress over dark hose and shiny black patent leather shoes. Her hair was chestnut, glossy, and hanging straight, parted on one side and pinned back with a tortoise-shell clasp. Her features were exotic and pretty, with narrow almond-shaped eyes, a straight sharp little nose, and a full mouth lipsticked soft pink. Her hair swung and flew as she moved about. Martin nearly grew dizzy watching her. "I hate driving in LA. How is San Diego?"

Martin shrugged and said blandly, "San Diego is home. Sunny, balmy, you know…"

"I would love to be there," Maritza said with a certain explosiveness. "I go there whenever I can to get away from here. My mother lives in a bungalow along the shore in La Jolla."

"Do you see much of Carol?"

"Carol Monegan?" Maritza looked surprised. "Oh yeah. We are old buddies, me and her. I have a string of friends in San Diego. I went to San Diego State for two years before changing to USC." She made a mysterious face. "My girlfriend is Scandinavian and athletic, so she drags me down to places like Solana Beach and Torrey Pines and Coronado to go surfing. I get to hang out with old friends, although I don't even know how to swim."

"I have never surfed in my life," Martin admitted. "Most of us in San Diego—the real San Diegans—if we're not devoted beach people—we may go look at the ocean once a year."

Maritza laughed. "I like that. My kind of guy."

They made small talk for a while, until—so it seemed to Martin—Maritza was comfortable with him and willing to take a chance referring him to some of the people in her network. Thank god for Carol and her idea. *Good idea*, Martin thought at last, no longer reluctant.

"There is a cattle drive this afternoon at the convention hall," Maritza admitted.

"I have my folder of résumés with me."

"Good man." Maritza sat down behind her cluttered, enormous glass-topped desk. She folded her hands over a stack of manila folders and manuscripts. Behind her, through half-shuttered plate glass windows, the skyline of Los Angeles brooded in an otherworldly light, almost apocalyptic. Much had been done to clean up the infamous smog of LA, which almost rivaled that of London a century earlier, but the air was still a bit of a stew. The roiling clouds, like on an alien planet, marinated in smoldering light colored like blood and lemon plasma, if there was such a thing.

Maritza said, "I have a proposition for you. I can get you in to see someone at the convention center."

"I'm open to anything," Martin said. "Thank you."

Maritza clapped her small, caramel hands together. Her fingers were little, which made her dark red fingernails look all the larger.

"Her name is Chloë, and she works for a rival of ours called Alienopolis."

"Intriguing name."

"Oh yes. They aim at a younger market in books, films, clothing, you name it."

"My friends and I are big Alienopolis fans and gamers," Martin said.

"That's our generation, honey." She shrugged. "Who knows. Chloë has been trying to convince me to move over there for two years now, but I have a certain loyalty factor. My employers value my loyalty and my talent, and pay me well to stay here. You on the other hand, Mr. Brown, require a little help getting a foot in the door. Carol made a good case for how nice and smart you are, so I want to help out in any way that I can."

"Wow, I'm touched." That small-town networking seemed to radiate across the globe—maybe the universe—from that little crab shack on the beach in PB.

"I owe Carol," Maritza said.

"I had no idea that Carol pulls so many strings."

Maritza sat back, with her hands folded in her lap, while her feet were raised on a slightly open middle drawer of the desk.

"Have you ever been to Surf & Turf Tap in Pacific Beach?"

"Several times," Maritza said. "I have the privilege of saying that I assisted a young lady in leaving her lunch on the sand in back after she drank a few margaritas too many."

"Anyone I know?" Martin asked cautiously.

"Probably. Carol's girlfriend Stephanie." Maritza paused. "Martin, I'm sorry. I thought you knew." Seeing his puzzled look—Martin had a sudden disoriented feeling—she added, "Carol is bi. I guess she doesn't spread the news around San Diego. You'll keep her secret, won't you?" She laughed. "Nothing is ever what it seems, eh?"

"Uh—yeah." It didn't matter to him. Carol was Carol. He'd known her since childhood, and it made no difference.

"Alicia is not, in case you are wondering." Maritza favored him with a sphinx-like look. "You guys are a wonderful little family down there, a Mafia of sorts. I love hanging out with Carol and Alicia and some of their crowd from Hillcrest and Coronado and La Jolla and whatnot." She rose and stuck her arm straight out, as if her hand were a switch on a railroad line, signaling that the interview was over.

"Good luck, Martin. If you say anything, I will deny it all."

"Mum's the word," he promised.

She saw him to the door (a huge mahogany-inlaid contraption, worthy of a spectacular film about ancient Egyptian pharaohs or something). There, she shook his hand again, wished him luck, and smiled after him as he walked down a hushed, carpeted hall big enough for a truck to drive down. It was lined with greenish, almost underwater plate glass windows, one after the other, overlooking a glowing reddish-yellow inferno in the LA atmosphere. It was like looking into a volcano. There was something mutely ominous about it. Martin could not put his finger on any sort of doom scenarios, but he was sure they were out there. It was Darwinian, like the screeching gulls in the parking lot at Arf & Scarf in PB.

Martin was sitting in a funny-smelling Uber, being driven by a quiet young man from Honduras who played classical music while reciting English lessons to himself. "How do you do, Mister Jones? Did you receive the order we sent? There should be fifty pounds of pork sausage suitable for large party pizzas. How is Mrs. Jones? I trust your stay at the hotel is first class. Do you like asparagus? I can recommend an excellent foot doctor. My wife has been taking classes in cooking. Do you know of a cure for bad breath?" He turned and said, "Excuse me, Sir, is bad breath the same as halitosis?"

Martin nodded. He politely did not comment on the fact that the driver must have eaten an entire sack of garlic for lunch, along with a ton of either cheese or old socks. "Yes," he said while holding his nose, pretending to make a joke, "halitosis is bad breath." In reality, he nearly passed out and would have fallen out of the back door. Luckily, he was able to roll the window down and pretend to be looking around at buildings outside, while taking deep, desperate gasps of outside air. Suddenly the LA smog was somehow almost fragrant.

What's a little smog among friends? he asked in his mind of nobody in particular. *Could be burned toast or smoldering tires. Good for ya. Anything but this breath of death.*

Martin was happy and relieved when he was able with shaky knees to step out of the Uber while the soft strains of Mozart and mozzarella wafted away in downtown traffic.

Ah, the small things in life—fresh air!—suddenly such joy.

As Martin stood on the crowded sidewalk outside the convention center, a young, Hispanic-looking policeman amid the crowd stepped close to Martin and asked, "Are you okay, buddy? You look a bit pale."

Martin nodded. "I was practicing holding my breath. I've done it ever since I was a little kid, whenever I get nervous. I'm afraid I got carried away."

"You do that a lot," said the cop, "and you will get carried away: to the emergency room."

"I'll do my best, officer."

"This is LA, sir, the big city. Anything is possible. Don't be nervous, and you'll be fine."

"Thank you for your kindness," Martin said fervently.

The officer nodded and backed away, leaving a sense of order.

Martin strode into the grand, cavernous hall. As expected, he was overwhelmed by the presence of thousands of young men and women in business suits, looking sharp and efficient as they strode around waving résumés like meat cleavers.

According to a large sign at the entrance, the hall had about six hundred participating companies. Most were from the Los Angeles area, but some were from other cities, a few even in Canada or Mexico. One row of tables hosted companies from Europe and Asia, and a few in Africa. Most of the companies were looking for computer programmers, engineers, and technical writers. The air above the tables was filled with colorful signs, balloons, even a pair of smallish blimps advertising an obscure but probably giant tech company. Some of the signs were in Chinese—*intriguing, but not a likely match for me*, Martin thought.

Martin found a section in one corner with mostly publishing and film industry reps at various tables. He recognized the names of several leading print magazines as well. Applicants formed lines in all directions, as they waited patiently to speak with men and women in business suits. Martin felt a bit overwhelmed by the noise, the crowd, even the mixture of perfumes and aftershaves that wafted through the air. He actually rather longed for the peace and quiet of his room at home, where he could work on the Fairly Great or at least the Acceptable American Novel. That was by now several thousand pages of notes, five hundred pages of narrative, two hundred pages of dialogue, and some sixty named characters that required a road map to track. He kept adding and building, so that it was becoming a kind of Andean mountain chain. His plan was to chop it up—possibly into a trilogy or a quartet or even a quintet.

An hour and a half later, along with several coffees, the Los Angeles atmosphere above the glasshouse ceilings of the convention center began to glow as if a silent atomic bomb full of burning tomatoes had exploded. Ordinary people's skin began to glow as well, reflecting that ominous, bloody light outside. It made one's skin look radiation-burned. And yet people didn't seem to notice. A sensitive poetic guy like Martin could stand there while that ocean of ambition, greed, desperation, and bad taste (breath?) swirled around him in a gyre. Where in all of this did he belong? He was having an existential hour, questioning whether he even wanted to stay in this city overnight. He had already blown a large mega-bucks wad on the plane and the Uber. What if he spent the hotel money on a train home instead? He was happy he had not tried driving his tired Elantra all the way here and back, to wrestle with traffic, parking, carjacking, and who knows what.

Maritza had given him a slip of paper, on which she had written a table number (39) and a time to meet Chloë Setreal. He stood staring at that beautiful, exotic-sounding name, written in Maritza's exquisite handwriting. For a few moments, he was lost in admiration—of Maritza's blue gel pen, with its rounded top loops and closely arrayed vertical slopes. Maritza was the sort of writer who could make anything look dramatic and important.

Ah, silly me. Dangerous me.

He had nearly failed to notice that the time for his meeting with Chloë Setreal was a few minutes away. He felt so overwhelmed in this place that he'd become a bit muzzy. Probably needed some lunch. He had not eaten since breakfast. If he missed that appointment, then he'd have wasted his time coming here. Not only would Maritza be mad at him, but so would Carol whose intimate secrets Maritza had blabbed. He wondered if Alicia knew. Of course she must. Ah, the secrets of SoCal…It was time to meet Chloë Setreal at Table 39.

He made his way through the din and the pressing crowd among all sorts of table numbers until finally there it was—could it just be another number, or did it have magical or shaman powers? Could it change his life? Anything was possible…Except what happened next: He met Chloë Setreal, and his life changed forever.

Chapter 3. Chloë Setreal

Chloë Setreal took his breath away when he first saw her. Martin still had a few copies of his resume in hand as he made his way through the throng. There it was: Table 39, Alienopolis's venue at the annual convention, cattle call, hiring spree, call it what you wish. He was supposed to meet this person—a Chloë Setreal—at this place and time.

All he saw was more books, more posters, more film clips flickering on wall displays, more clever blimps and dangling dominoes (almost like fuzzy dice in gang member cars), and of course eager, desperate job-seekers.

Table 39 was actually several folding tables end to end, with white tablecloths over them, and stacks of product. That included the latest action figures, because Alienopolis specialized in gaming and fantasy adventure books to match the games and their spinoffs. Martin had played the games online with his buddies and knew all of the leading characters from the upper-level game, called Empire of Time, on down to spun-off subworlds. All together, they styled it the Alienopolis World. Its capital was Meta4City, in which lived the Royalty of the Empire of Time, spanning billions of years and billions of light years of the cosmos—past, present, future, and Other. Mix together the atmosphere of Gotham, the heroics and fluttering capes of Super Guys, the Arthurian swords and plumed helmets of High Fantasy, the deep space *sigh-fie* of Galactic War Trek and Far Wreck. Add hot warrior chicks with bulging tits and rippling muscles, waving impossibly huge swords; brooding Gothic monks and nuns; throw in a half dozen other well-reviewed product ingredients—and you had the Alienopolis product line, or most of it. There was always something more.

Number 39 was the only table at the convention so utterly swarmed by people of all ages, seeking to be near their passion. At one end of the table stood several living, breathing action figures from the game, including King Hawfar, Queen Ginger Beer, Sir Laugh-a-Lot, the Duke of Url, the Dike of Holland, and Princess Krashdisk, among others who milled about outside a row of changing room dividers.

It took Martin a minute or so to realize that the divine being who stood at the other end of the table was not an action figure but an employee of Alienopolis. She was young, beautiful, and fresh. She was slim, with a belly at once flat yet soft, athletic and feminine, strong yet vulnerable. She stood with sandy-colored hands loosely interlocked over the midsection of her black dress, beaming at the passion and interest exhibited by swarming fans. Her name tag read *Chloë.*

She was The One. Martin's heart sank with melancholy, intoxicated with longing, drunk with the agonizing cross-pleasures of desire and denial. This was the girl you could not have. She was either married, or going steady, or there must be some other reason why—the timing was off, she thought you were too ugly or too broke or whatever. Martin usually did okay with women—notwithstanding his recent breakup in Berkeley—and there was always the next one. But then there was always that elusive movie-star level beyond which the average guy must not strive. This chick was in the stratosphere. He was already disappointed.

As he focused on her, Chloë Setreal became aware of his stare. Their gazes interlocked and became a single laser beam of concerted energy, enough to power an Empire of Time planet. They were transported to Meta4City, where (as the game slogans said) adventure lurked in the shadows, romance bloomed over moonlit deserts, and Knights of Good rode out to battle the Evils of Night.

She turned to him, with her hands still linked over her belly, and blinked maybe once or twice. "You must be Mr. Brown." Her voice had a rich, sweet musicality, like honey drizzling over cinnamon rolls, or whipped heavy cream snowing on juicy peaches. She wore her dark, lustrous brown hair in a page boy cut, like an athlete—parted over the top of a beautifully shaped head with a high, intelligent forehead and a sharply inked, proportionately small but perfectly chiseled lower face. Her skin was a shade between honey and caramel—Mediterranean meets Baltic, purr-meets-fection, and *wow does that rock.* Her attractiveness was a mix of beauty and handsome, with a strong little square chin, short bony jawline sloping inward, that ripe full ironic mouth, and a straight little airbrushed nose. Those eyebrows—they were like a thunderstorm of smarts and sarcasm, gathered over the blue skies of her eyes, ready to wrinkle at you if you said something dumb.

What is it about her? Martin could only stop in his tracks and stare. Were you allowed to speak with a person of such grace and perfection?

Her mouth formed a candy-apple red equal sign; no, actually, it was not an equal sign but one of those double ($\approx$) sorta-equal signs, a wry twist that layered a delicious mix of gamine and humor over her prettiness. Below that intelligent forehead, and below those large deeply azure-blue eyes, she was graced with a tapering lower face that imposed sharp, boyish lines on soft, feminine curves (just talking about her facial features, not even her body yet). She did not look at you so much as she lowered and aimed those eyebrows and that forehead at you, and looked into your soul with those San Diego sky eyes, perfect darkish blue without a cloud in them (unless your reflection in them was a puff of cloud).

Martin's eyes were so locked in on her features that he had to force himself to look down, up, down, and up again.

Chloë lowered her forehead at him, looked at him with those analytical, skeptical eyes, and managed a laugh. "Mr. Brown?"

She appeared as startled by him as he was by her. The eyebrows jumped slightly back, like cats that wanted to be petted, but were suddenly spooked. They'd come back to try again, no worry.

He joked, "I came to rescue you."

"Oh?" She laughed. "Someone sent you to rescue me?" When she laughed, her upper lip pulled back, revealing a butcher block of small, perfectly aligned, bluish-white teeth. Firm cheeks pulled up under small but solid cheekbones. She probably ran the mile in under {*plug in a number,* Martin thought} and was naturally competitive in track or fencing or who knows what. She was, in a word, imposing; a normal, thoughtful guy would think twice before risking his delicate ego on that cutting board. But she came across as kind and gentle, without high maintenance or complex emotional machinery. She handled herself like a Harley. When you're that good, you don't need to huff or puff. You just ride. The highway will fall in line behind you. So it appeared to be with Chloë Setreal. "Do I need rescuing?"

"Of course. That's why they sent me."

"They?" She appeared relaxed and seemed to be enjoying herself, going along with the program.

"Maritza Dusenbery."

"Oh yes, they." She put her index finger over her lips. "She whose name must not be uttered."

"That's the one. She told me to give you this." He handed her a copy of his résumé.

Chloë took it, respectfully pretending to take him seriously, and glanced at the single page of print. "Great American Novel. Very impressive."

"It doesn't say that." He added, "yet."

"It will. Maritza called me and warned me that I would be rescued. She described you as a tall, dark, handsome man wearing a cape."

"Obviously, I came disguised."

"And very cleverly so, Mr. Brown."

"I am the mild-mannered reporter, Martin Brown, working for the Daily Surf & Turf."

"The *what*?"

"Secret spot in Pacific Beach. Steamers on the half shell, craft beer, you should try it some time."

"I might just do that one day, if the right person came to rescue me."

"I thought you were one of the actors."

"Now, Mr. Brown, do I look like a stand-in? Should I be upset?"

"Not at all. I took you for Queen Ginger Beer."

"You mean Guinevere."

"That one."

"Oh, Mr. Brown, I think we have much to talk about."

"I would agree. I must interrogate you properly over lunch. Do you take your carbs with cola or root beer?"

"Diet. Anything."

"Of course. The slender figure."

She stepped out from behind the table so that he could see her fully for the first time. He was in love. She was a combination of girl next door and rock star.

"I took you for one of the producers," she said.

They stood for a full minute, lost in each other, and admiring one another. Martin found her to be elegant, Continental, sophisticated, educated—yet relaxed, easy-going, generous with her manners and emotions. He wondered how he looked to her.

She told him, an hour later, over Japanese food at a little glass and steel ultra-modern place near the UCLA campus. Martin and Chloë sat side by side at a white bar overlooking three people in blue paper Samurai hats, who rolled fresh sushi by hand to order. They looked lost and anonymous amid reflections and glass surfaces in which their images did or did not appear. It was kind of cool, Martin thought, spotting himself alone in one window, her alone in another window, and both of them together in a third window—and nobody in yet a fourth window. Martin reflected on cosmological questions. Could you exist in all windows at the same time, or was each a life lived in a parallel universe without reference or indexing to the others?

Does a person not reflected in a window actually exist?

Outside, the Los Angeles planet atmosphere turned Jupiter with red and yellow stripes. The thick air seemed to be on fire, except it was a non-consuming, cool dream-fire. People and cars moved through the air outside as if through soup and irony.

Inside, it was air conditioned and rather cold. Chloë had driven them here in her little older-model Volkswagen, which was white as snow, its taillights sprinkled with tiny flower motifs. She had donned a mossy-green, soft corduroy blazer that complimented her black dress in an odd way—just as boyish and girlish themes criss-crossed on the surface of her elegant, warm personality.

"You look very natural with your chopsticks," he said inside.

They sat so close they could murmur to each other.

"Pass the green mustard, please, Martin."

"How about some soy sauce for your Tuna Treasure?" It was a house theme, apparently, to create a game of Asian pirates, as in Tuna Treasure, Clam Chest, Sword Fish; what else? Martin flipped through the menu—Dessert Island—all so original, he thought sarcastically.

She choked back a quick laugh. "You have a way of saying things."

"I try to say things."

"You do," she said, caught in mid-mouthful. She was one of these people who wave their fingers over their mouth if they talk while eating—apparently, so you cannot see into their mouth, and get grossed out by rice and tuna and spit and seaweed (*see* weed?) going *glop, glop* on the person's tongue like icky paste. "I like it. You make everything sound sort of sarcastic and funny."

"It is my natural sense of tragedy, living with the inevitable but still hoping for the evitable, and settling for something edible like this incredible but ridiculous fish food."

"You are a riot," she said, bumping her shoulder against his as one could only do in a tiny restaurant where you sat closer than sardines in can. In a city where real estate was really pricey, that made a lot of sense. In laid back San Diego, it would raise eyebrows.

She added, "it's nice that they don't just call it fish." She made a New
York hoodlum voice and said, "Hey, youse getcha fish here on da
dock. Bring yer own foahk or eat witcha hands. We don't give a shit."

It was Martin's turn to nearly choke. "You *are* an actress. I
knew it."

"I lived in Noo-Yawk for a few yehyohs whilst I was porking
moy core."

"You're too young to be Queen Gingivitis. I'd say you are more
like Princess Baby Teeth."

"I'm not that young, Martin. I am old enough to be your
mother."

"Oh really. I am twenty-two. How old of a wizened old prune
are you?"

"Twenty-three, Junior. Have some respect."

"I have respect. I am in awe."

"Aw, shucks. Awe what?"

"I am just—how do I say?"

"*Je ne sais pas. Je ne sais quoi.*" I don't know. I don't know
what. She made a groping motion in mid-air with one hand, as if
looking for the elusive whatsis she could not quite put her finger on.

*Jawohl, Schatzi, und heute ist Samstag, so müssen wir den
Rasen mähen.* "Yes, Sweetie, and today is Saturday, so we have to
mow the lawn." Textbook German like you study in high school. He
had spent some time in Germany, and spoke the language fairly
fluently, so the textbook speech was a put-on. She got the joke,
looking totally comfortable and unintimidated.

"*Vous êtes quoi? Fou?*" You are what? Nuts?

"*Ich bin ganz nüchtern and schüchtern.*" I am very sober and
shy.

"I love when you talk dirty to me."

"That's not dirty, it's Deutsch."

"*Jahha-ha,*" she drawled. "You love to rhyme things."

He put his hand on her back and was pleased that she pressed
back with a surprisingly delicate little shoulder blade under that thin,
dark corduroy material. She was strong and wiry to the touch, yet
feminine and adorable.

"I was saying, *ma chère…*"

"So you do speak French," she said feigning playful outrage,
"and you understood all the provocative things I said about you."

He made a passionate, adoring face, tilting his head to one side.

"I loved every one of your charming, intimate little syllables. Please, tell me more things…"

She placed a chopstick pinch of California roll over those red lip slivers masking a lush, full mouth. Up came the shielding fingers. "You want me to tell you a story?"

"Yes. The three bears."

"Maybe later, if you are nice and take me for a walk."

Her eyes twinkled as she ate. Pause *reparté*, they silently agreed.

After dinner, they sauntered arm in arm down crowded streets filled with tourists.

Darkness fell amid a fireball of planetary sunlight that soaked Westwood Village and its environs in alien twilight. The planet seemed to roll in a sauce of lava. And yet nobody was burning, because they were native to this ecosphere like certain oddly shaped deep-sea urchins like to flutter across the mulmy plains of the abyssal deep, or high-flying eagles with white crew cuts brave the thin, cold air around the highest mountain peaks.

"Earth," Martin said. "Good place to call home."

She slipped a hand and strong little arm around his back and pulled tightly. "You say the strangest things, Martin."

"I do it all for you."

She laid her cheek against his chest as they walked. "I thought you were a producer."

He gave her opposite shoulder bone a quick rub. "You say that often, and wistfully."

She spoke into his jacket in a muffled voice. "Mixed emotions."

He stopped and took her in both arms, almost as if they were slow dancing. She returned his gesture, linking her hands at the small of his back while looking up at him (a four-inch difference in altitudes, a meeting of attitudes) with sincere, pleading eyes. "Martin?"

"Yes, dear?" He looked down, loving her eyebrows, her forehead, those serious blue eyes, that strong little face.

"Martin..." She reached up and brushed fingers lightly over his forehead, combing a few stray hairs away. He waited. She said, "This town is full of producers and..."

"And? Yes?"

She spoke hesitantly, unburdening her soul. "You know this is called the City of Angels." It was a question.

"I have found only one, and that is you."

"You are so sweet." She lingered for a moment on the last syllable, adoring him. "You bring a flavor with you of a different place..."

"Je ne sais quoi," he said helpfully. *I don't know what.*

She pulled her hands back, then raised them to hold his face gently between her palms. "Sometimes, Martin, this really seems like the City of Assholes."

"My CPU is processing. Please stand by."

She giggled. "I see your brain spinning behind those lovely brown eyes. Your computer will process for a long time. Let me help you understand. This is the Big City."

"I'm not going to say what rhymes with that."

"You don't need to." She placed one hand on his shoulder in a companion fashion, while stroking his ear, his cheek, his neck with the other hand so he got goosebumps. "There are producers everywhere, and they produce a lot of bullshit."

From her tone, he could read she'd had a bad experience with such a manure farmer.

She laid her cheek against his chest. "Are you real, Martin?"

He held her close, rocking her gently. "What you see is what you get. That's our product guarantee."

She made a faint mewling sound, like a kitten. "I believe you. I'm a fool, but I want to trust you."

He gently raised that small, square chin with a crooked index finger.

"Don't say it." Her eyes as she looked up suddenly were wide, and filled with drizzle. It was a rainy, cloudy, windy sky with fleeting clouds and flashes of lightning. It was a silent movie, so you could not hear thunder growling. "Just hold me." She laid her cheek back on his chest and snuggled.

He wrapped her in his embrace, and emoted all the love he could. He waited, only fanning his fingers gently over the sharp ridges of her shoulderblades. In his heart, at that moment, he knew he would love this woman for every moment in the rest of his life—whether she let him or not.

He adored her little fists, which awkwardly made kneading motions against his collarbones, as if they were mulling over thoughts.

He wanted to tell her—but she said not to say anything—that he almost hadn't come to LA but Carol Monegan and Alicia Washington had talked—no, badgered—him into it. He had come here not as a producer or an asshole, and not even expecting much, unlike those desperate young men and women in business suits at the cattle drive. He had been thinking of taking the train home rather than staying the night. He wanted to tell her that she was a sleeper, a keeper, a finder, a blinder, but he just stayed silent and slow-danced with her—almost—just rocking her gently. Was she crying? He couldn't tell. Was he in danger of having his heart stolen and destroyed by some female LA producer asshole whatever? This could work both ways.

"Sorry," she suddenly said. "Walk me to my car. Please." Her eyes were troubled, looking elsewhere, deep underwater, into the past, with a look on her face that was almost apologetic.

"Sure."

They held hands and walked slowly back along Westwood Plaza with its little trees lining the center divide, and alternating big office buildings and blocks of small shops.

He wasn't going to push. He was so totally open to whatever might happen, and she was so stratospheric that he didn't dare think he might see her again. He was prepared for it to have been a wonderful, memorable hour or two with some nice laughs and conversation.

"I have your résumé," she said as they swung their clasped hands playfully between them. "I will make sure and get that to someone in Creative who will give you a fair shot. That's the best I can do."

"That's more than I dare to ask."

"I'm not a big-shot, just a girl in an office building."

"You are the nicest thing that's happened to me here in Los

Angeles."

She squeezed his hand. "You too."

Stunned, he mulled that over. Questions whizzed over his head like shooting stars on a summer night.

"I hate to cut it short, but I am due at a wedding reception in the morning."

"Not your own."

"No, Mr. Sarcastic." She jumped up on tiptoes and kissed him on the mouth, a quick moist swipe full of affection. "One of the *producers*."

"Oh, those."

"Yeah."

"I'm afraid to ask."

"Don't."

"That bad?"

"Yeah." They walked for a while, holding hands. "Will you come and walk with me again?"

They were just passing a store window full of magazines. A hundred beautiful, smiling women with white teeth, red lips, and wonderful eyes beamed at them.

He stopped and held her. "I would be honored. And it would be really, really cool if you could drop by San Diego sometime. I'd love to take you to the beach, feed you crabs and beer, we can see the zoo and Balboa Park..."

"You don't have anyone in your life right now, huh?"

He shook his head.

She said, "It's been a while for me too. I don't know if I am ready to open up quite yet." She patted his chest thoughtfully with her palm. "Martin."

"Mmh?"

"Oh, Martin." She sounded so wistful and forlorn.

No joking now.

He knew in his heart that his life and hers depended on being serious.

She rubbed his chest with her palm, as if erasing something at that spot in preparation for writing something new—over his heart. "What I meant was. When I said producer. I meant that you have this air about you of someone very important and very sincere. I think I had a crush on you from the first moment I saw you and you were looking at me like that."

"Me too."

"Looking at me in that tone of voice," she joked, but faintly.

He took her hands in his and gently squeezed to reassure her—and himself. She squeezed back. Her eyes looked up into his.

She asked, "You're going back tonight?"

He nodded, reluctantly. "Yes." He wanted to stay with her, and the idea of being here in LA alone, separated from her, was not something he wanted to imagine. Better to get home, on familiar turf, catch his breath, gather his thoughts (and his sanity), and reset. Reboot.

"I hope we see each other again," she said.

"I believe we will. I want to."

"I do too."

He walked her to her car, where they stood for a time embracing and deeply kissing. He thought making love with her would be like this—the perfect fit of their mouths together, their tongues wriggling with pleasure and passion as they sought each other in the intimacy of that liquid, mucous environment, that sharing of so much.

He waved, forlorn and heroic, as she drove away in the white VW Beetle.

Was that shock on her face, were those tears, was that a look of loss? Or was it hope?

He called for an Uber and told the middle-aged driver, a man with gray hair and beard stubble, to drop him off at the train station. It would be a long, thoughtful ride south along the sea, amid a blur of city lights like in Santa Monica and Long Beach, Dana Point and San Clemente, and ultimately San Diego.

The thing he'd wanted to say to her—but didn't get a chance to—was, *I came here expecting nothing, and you gave me the world. Even if we never see each other again, you gave me two wonderful hours that recharged the batteries of my soul. I will never forget you. But I hope I don't need to. Just call, and I'll drive on up there. It's just two hours and some change, after all. Just two little hours separating us—not even one full tank of gas or need to stop for coffee… so please call if you feel like it. I do.*

As Martin dozed on the train, he half expected a sweet little text message or something maybe like *Miss you already.*

Nothing came. His cell phone stayed dead.

Chapter 4. San Diego Interlude

Martin Brown held a coffee cup in one hand and his cell phone in the other, as he sprawled on one of the big black leather easy chairs in his parents' den. A news program ran on the big-screen TV, with the sound off and some story running about people harvesting oranges in Israel.

"Martin!" his mother called from the kitchen.

"Mom!" he bellowed, shaking the phone—which had stopped working.

"Do as your mother says," his dad chided from the distant home office, where he conducted semi-retired real estate banking.

"Loser!" Debbie chimed in from outside. Martin's younger sister, an attractive brunette presently wearing a pink bikini, sat by the backyard pool, tanning herself on a lawnchair.

Martin held the phone in both hands, close to his mouth as if to eat it, and said, "I can't stay here anymore. They are driving me insane."

"Martin!" his mother called. "Can you move the car and get the groceries out of the back before the ice cream melts? All you do is sit and watch TV all day."

"I'm recovering from final exams!" Martin cried while raising his face and both arms to the ceiling.

No need to dwell on the scene. Day by day, the drama played out thus.

Martin met Joe Logan at the Surf & Turf Tap at one in the afternoon. It was still sunny, but a storm was moving in from the Pacific Ocean. Out on the beach, surfer dicks & chicks stood with their hair blowing to one side as they held their boards and looked out to sea. Life guards drove up and down the beach in orange combat vehicles, speaking on megaphones. Martin could not make out the words, just the tone. Whatever they were saying sounded ominous if not apocalyptic.

It was comfortable inside the bar. Martin wore a grayish-white hoodie. Joe wore sweats. Joe's hair looked wet and tousled from a long set on the swells (Martin's language for *Joe had been surfing since daybreak*).

Joe looked tanned, fit, and relaxed. "Four-foot rollers from the southwest all morning," Joe said as he held a cold beer. He had showered, and changed into a dark red sweat suit with the SDSU slogan down one leg. He was about to become a senior at San Diego State University. "What's the matter with you?"

Martin fingered a hot cup of tea in both hands. "I am thinking of moving to London."

"Really," Joe said, leaving the floor open for Martin to elaborate.

The interior was, as always, shady and hospitable. It was like the weather—a lowlying babble of conversation, covered by a high layer of darkness and peace under the beamed ceilings. The walls all around were decorated with surf photos and other souvenirs dating back half a century—smiling men and women in grayscale, proud of their trophies, showing off their swimsuits and ripped bodies.

"Home life," Martin said as if that explained everything. "I am not going to live at home next summer. I probably won't make it through this summer."

"London," Joe repeated while crouched around his beer at the bar with both muscular arms wrapped around the glass as if he were a large cat, and the beer was a kill he was about to enjoy.

"Oh yeah. London. It's an option. I just wonder if it's far enough away."

"Ulan Bator," Joe suggested.

"What?"

"Outer Mongolia."

"No Mexican food."

"That's true," Joe said. "But we had a surfer chick at State from there. She could slide rings around any guy. I dated her while she went to State. Nice girl."

At that moment, Martin's phone made a flushing-toilet sound, gurgling at length.

> You have one unread
> txt message.

He pressed TXT and read the message. It was from Alienopolis Meta4City 39. His heart nearly stopped, but slowly resumed its pounding beat. He had programmed her name in code. That was Chloë Setreal.

> Martin. How R U.

Joe said, "Bad news? You look like you just had a cow."

Martin shook his head. "Excuse me." He rose, took his tea, and walked out the front door while finger-tipping a reply.

> Fine & U?

The reply came back two long minutes later. She must have been typing.

> Newses(2). Had
> accident last night but
> going 2 B OK. Set up
> interv 4 U. Cn U come 2
> LA?

He tipped back,

> OGY. Call?

She replied,

> Will call U 4 pm. Pls B 4
> Me.

He replied,

Always 4 U.

She did not answer. He let the phone slide into one of the
pockets on his hoodie. In his mind, he kept the conversation going.
OGY meant *Oh God Yes*. He wanted to add but didn't,

F
Y
A

For You Anything. He was terrified she would think it meant
For Your Ass, and decided not to—that would be pushing things.

"Hey." Joe came outside, holding his beer, and sat down at the
table with Martin. "What are you up to? Looks like that tea woke you
up. What's in that?"

Martin felt a glow of joy inside. Was it possible that his summer
and his life had been rescued? Was he about to have a new love life
with the most wonderful and amazing chick he'd ever met?

"You're on drugs," Joe guessed.

"No, I'm in love."

"That will do it every time. Can you drive home safely?"

"I'm not going home."

"Ever again?"

"I am going to LA."

Joe gave him a perplexed look, filled with concern. "Dude"

Martin shook his head. "I'll be fine, but thanks for your concern.

Joe sat back, tanned and blond, with his rough, weathered hands
linked over his taut abdomen. "Who's the woman?"

"Girl that Carol and Alicia turned me on to. Works for
Alienopolis in Los Angeles."

Joe brightened. "I know of them. They publish games and
novels and movies about a bunch of superheroes and weird
characters."

"I know," Martin said. "It's my only hope in life as a writer. If
I can get into the industry, which is like one chance in a million, I
will revel and dwell in a fantasy world beyond anything we can
imagine."

"True," Joe said. "I've played the role of Captain Tibur, the
Shark King. I lead ninety-nine prehistoric sharks on a crusade under

the sea to fight evil and save beautiful chicks. It's really cool."

Martin nodded and imitated Joe's posture, looking more academic and less athletic. What the hell—Chloë was a goddess, and she had liked him the way he was. "To hell with Shakespeare and Tolstoy. They had their day. We live in the age of Alienopolis superheroes and duperheroines."

"You are on a roll," Joe said admiringly. "When do you start?"

"I'm not that far along," Martin admitted. "I have to run up to LA for an interview. I don't know. Chloë is handling the details."

"Chloë," Joe said in a questioning tone. "Your new secretary?"

"My duper heroine."

"Lucky you." He rose. "Well, I gotta split. I'm tending bar at the Surf Board up in Del Mar starting today. Did I tell you?"

"No, but congrats, man."

"Yeah, thanks. It's four nights a week. My new summer gig. Drop by some time."

"I will."

"When you're not chasing phantoms in Hollywood or whatever." Joe paused briefly to look around. "Enjoy the last of this warm, sunny weather for the next few days. It's going to be wet and windy."

Martin sat at the table a while, as Joe strode off to climb into a rusting but chopped and cool VW Beetle classic and rattled off in a cloud of blue smoke toward Coastal Highway 101 going north.

He called home to tell his sister to tell his parents he might be out really late. He didn't confide about Los Angeles. Too many questions, too much excitement, too little time.

"I'll tell them," his little sister said. He could detect her sneer without seeing her.

"Out here," Martin signed off, wondering if he and she could ever be friends. And she was a really smart, cute girl. But so spoiled. Aside from being deathly loyal to one another, they had hated each other for over twenty years. Why change anything now?

At four p.m., Martin sat in a diner near the Old Town, San Diego entrance ramp to I-5 pointing north toward Los Angeles. He was seated at a table with the remnants of a barbecue beer dinner with mashed potatoes and veggies (peas and carrots), reading a Wall Street Journal someone had left behind, and sipping coffee. At 4:05 his phone made flushing sounds. This time, it was a phone call rather than a text message.

His throat constricted anxiously. "*Halurf?*" he croaked.

"Martin?"

"*Yrk.*"

"Is that Martin Brown?"

He cleared his throat. "Yes." He added in a voice filled with wonder, "Chloë."

"I'm so glad to be talking with you," she said in a tone that suggested he was a life raft and she was a survivor of a sinking ocean liner.

"Me too." He hoped he sounded fairly casual—not too eager, but then again not like he didn't care.

"Oh, Martin."

"What is this about an accident?"

"I was driving away from you last night, wishing I didn't have to go, and I got T-boned by a drunk driver. Luckily not too hard. It was like some sort of karma stepped in."

"You didn't really want to go to that wedding."

"No." She laughed, but her laugh was cut short. "Ouch. It hurts to laugh."

"Are you okay?"

"I have three cracked ribs, a bruised face, and a broken femur in my left leg."

"Oh my god."

"I will live, Martin. I will live to have sushi with you again in that place with the windows and the green mustard that turns your breath into dragon flames."

"At least you still have your sense of humor."

"It's not broken," she agreed in a sort of purr from the back of her throat. "How are you?"

"Thinking of you."

"Oh, how sweet. Oh, Martin."

"Sweetie, you said that before."

"And I'll say it again."

"And I'll gladly listen. Oh, Chloë."

"Now you're making fun of me," she teased.

"No, I have a younger sister I do that with. I can have, like, real human-to-human contact with you instead of human-to-alien or human-to-zoo."

"I guess it's rough. I was an only child."

"Does that make you an only person now that you're grown up?"

"That's what I adore about you—so philosophical."

"Not a producer."

"Thank heavens. Hey, I put in a good word for you."

"Bless you."

"I'd like you to be in LA where I can see you."

"That would be so nice."

"Ouch. Sorry. It hurts when I move. Martin, this is serious. I spoke to one of the Alienopolis producers, and they are very interested in having you on board as a creative writer. I'm going to put $400 in your bank account to cover travel and expenses."

"No."

"I'm serious. These people really want to interview you."

"Oh my god."

"So I hope to see you when?" She laughed. "Later this evening, if you can swing it?"

"Oh god yes. Are you home?"

"I am in my apartment off Wilshire Boulevard, by the UCLA campus near where we had sushi. My two girl roommates are in and out. One of them is a grad student of film, and the other is a nursing student. I'm the oddball because I work for a living, and I will probably forever be three credits shy of my English degree."

"You're kidding. Another English major."

"There is hope for us."

"Can you use some company?"

"Of course, if you don't mind being around an invalid."

"You are the older woman in my life right now."

"By what, a few months?"

"I calculated when you told me. I think you are eight months older than I am."

"You are a child. Yes, I think I am an only person. But not a lonely person. I have you."

"How sweet. I am prepared to drive up there if that's okay."

"I would *lo-ove* the company, Martin. I promise not to whine."

"It's okay if you do—a little bit."

"I'll keep it to a low, drawn-out moaning sound."

"Thank you. Can I bring anything? Flowers? Chocolate?"

"You."

"Aw."

"You might have to run out for some take-out. I can't move much, so I will be a lousy hostess. I'm sitting here in this plush old chair with my left leg in a cast, propped up on a wooden chair. I have my bedroom pillows on either side of me because my ribs are killing me. Actually, it only hurts when I move, or even think of moving."

"I cracked a rib once in high school karate class. No fun."

"Are you a black belt?"

"I never got past white. I became interested in track. I did come in first a few times in events."

"That is why you look so fit."

He said, "The primary skill of a martial artist is to run like hell when meeting idiots on the street. It's not about ego but about survival."

"Spoken like a prehistoric mammal."

"I am that, and more."

"I can't wait to see you."

"Me neither."

"I'll be watching old black and white movies and wishing you were here already. Be safe, okay?"

"Wouldn't that be a trip, us each sitting there with a broken leg up."

"Don't even joke about it. I want you here in one piece so I can hug you, my teddy bear."

"Oh my god, my fur is just tingling at the thought of getting strokes."

"We can have cookies and milk together. You have to stop to pick them up."

"Fair deal. What do you like?"

"I'm easy. Chocolate chip. Nothing fancy."

"My kind of girl."

"I'd love to be."

"Can't wait to see you. Like two hours, probably, if there's no traffic."

"I hear there is a big storm coming. Do be careful."

"Neither rain nor sleet will keep me from worshiping at your feet."

"Drive safely."

"I have a question to ask when I get there."

"Really?"

"Yes. Don't answer—but why do you have an umlaut over your *e*?"

"That's not an umlaut, my sweet darling baby prince. I'll explain everything when you get here."

"Oh, Chloë, I can't wait.

"Oh, Martin."

They each breathed a fond *bye* and rang off.

Martin walked on air as he hurried to his car for a quick ride to LA.

Chapter 5. Stormy Beach

With a full tank of gas, and a full stomach, Martin Brown steered his white Elantra onto I-5 and blended into traffic. It looked like a smooth drive.

The sun set as Martin left San Diego behind.

To his left, over the glittering sea, a massive wall of dark-bluish-black cloud moved in. All that was left of the day was a thin ribbon of light stretching from one end of the horizon to the other. In the midst of that, the sun sank like a giant yellow egg yolk swimming in reddish cocktail sauce. All that was needed now were a bowl of giant shrimps or crab cocktail. Martin grinned at this cleverness. He had eaten and, if anything, he might grab another cup of coffee along the way, but he felt upbeat and good and happy. *Wow.* What a beautiful, wonderful girl this Chloë was. And why did she have the two little dots over her *e* if they weren't an umlaut as in German?

He daydreamed as he drifted along in a current of ruby red taillights.

A little bit north of Carlsbad but still south of San Onofre, he heard a clanking, clattering noise somewhere deep in the bowels of the car.

Oh my lord now what?

The oily gods of the machine were going to rain on his parade.

The clattering sound got worse.

He drove past a sign that read, *You are leaving San Diego County.*

Moments later, a second sign passed by, which read, *Welcome to Orange County.*

Reluctantly, he fought his way over to the right lane and pulled over onto the shoulder.

The first stinging pits of drizzle began to pepper his face as he got out and started a walk-around inspection. A cold, damp wind set in. The sun was just about gone now.

He could not see anything immediately, obviously wrong. He knew virtually nothing about cars. The tires were inflated and looked good. He crouched low and stared under the car in the failing light. Nothing was dripping. He sniffed, and could not detect any oily or burning or other weird smells that shouldn't be.

He heard himself emit a single sob of utter frustration. He could be in LA intwo hours with the dream of his life, and here he was on a grimy freeway, smelling the exhaust of a million cars, and weeping with the melancholy secrets of myriad red warning lights heading who knows where.

"This cannot be!" he shouted, raising his face and arms to the sky.

When he got in and started the car, it coughed and choked. It rattled reluctantly into life, like an animal in pain. He thought of Chloë with her leg up. Maybe the Elantra needed to have its leg up. Then the car died with a few last racking, wheezing shakes and moans. He could not get it going again. The starter barely coughed, but would not turn over.

Perplexed, he got out and scouted the landscape as twilight fell and a light drizzle grew.

How quickly one became soggy in the sleet, or was it tears streaming down one's cheeks?

A wind picked up as well. A large cardboard box flattened and mangled in traffic came twirling by in a slipstream of black exhaust fumes.

He spotted the next exit a short distance ahead. To the left, on the other side of the freeway toward the beaches and towns, he saw a cluster of bright lights. They advertised food, gas, lodging, and presumably comfort or at least car repairs. Who on earth would work on a car unexpectedly at this hour of evening? He had no choice—he must try.

He got the car started once again and crawled along the shoulder until he could roll down the exit. A few drivers honked at him in annoyance, but most people were understanding. He drove slowly, keeping his hazard flashers on to signal that he was having car trouble. At the bottom of the exit ramp, he rolled carefully through a stop sign and took a left. Rumbling and bucking, the car took him under an overpass, west down a hill into a coastal town he'd never heard of.

It looked sort of pretty, except for the ominous darkness of the storm. Lights spread out before him, and beyond that the dark line of the beach, and ultimately the gloomy smoke that was now a dark and stormy night full of rain and wind all the way out to sea. The horizon had become invisible. There wasn't a star to be seen. Droplets began to fall on the window, rolling down the glass. Rain went *pong, pong* on the metal roof.

Luckily, the road toward the beach went downhill. Droplets rattling on the roof were the only sound. The engine was dead. He was simply rolling.

Three roaring cars in a pack swerved around him with blaring horns as their drivers raced toward the beach.

He needed to get as far from the traffic as possible.

He also realized with a further sinking feeling that he couldn't even see the lights from that food-gas-lodging area. He was marooned in a small beach town on a stormy evening. Maybe he would bite the bullet and hire an Uber to drive him to the nearest bus or train station, and from there he could make his way to Los Angeles. It was a plan. Once in LA, he could Uber the last few miles to Chloë's apartment. It would give him a good excuse to spend the night, even if he had to sleep on the floor. Seeing her was the only thing he cared about, by hook or by crook.

He did have his cell phone. So he checked his location and, sure enough, he was pulled over at the curb overlooking a cul-de-sac that terminated at a row of concrete posts with heavy chains concatenated between each pair. He spotted a sandy space near the end of the street, and managed to get the car slowly rolling toward it. Even with the engine off, it made this clanking, grinding sound as if crocodiles were eating piles of empty tin cans.

He remembered that Joe Logan would be working at a bar this evening, not too far from here. But Joe would be tied up until the wee hours, so he kept that in reserve. Uber was now his best bet. He pressed the preset on his cell phone and waited. Nothing happened. He must be in a dead spot. If he went back to the top of the street, he might get the connection back on which he'd checked his GPS.

He did have a poncho in the trunk for occasions like this. He found a greasy old baseball cap in the back seat. That and the poncho would be his only protection against the elements. He checked to make sure he had his wallet in his back pocket. What else?

There was nothing else. There was only getting to LA now by any means possible.

So much for a quick two-hour ride. And some change.

Some change had turned into potential hours.

Nothing was going to keep him from finishing this trip. There would be milk and cookies at the end, and perhaps snuggling with his wounded friend. He daydreamed about how they would hold each other and never let go. They would whisper endearments and kiss each other's hands, one little finger at a time. The intoxication of infatuation warmed him inwardly like brandy after frigid hours of skiing, as he sometimes did in winter months at Mammoth or at Snow Mountain.

He got out of the car, slammed the door shut without locking it, and started to hike back up the sidewalk. He saw about five houses on this side of the street, and an equal number on the other side. Each seemed to have one dimly glowing window, snuggled secretively and privately among huge old cypress bushes and brush cherry hedges. The anatomy of the neighborhood was not hard to figure. Beach houses tended to be small. Property was very valuable. Many such places were rentals, occupied by young working people, owned by wealthy absentee landlords. This would be a typical street, with parking prohibited, and signs forbidding skateboards and other nuisances of summer tourism. Here, even San Diego residents were considered tourists and outsiders—if anyone even knew about a place like this. Locals would stroll down here on sunny days to walk on the beach, kick a foot into the surf, walk the dog, toss a stick, or stand gazing at distant ships.

Martin had not passed the first house, the first glowing window shrouded in cypresses, when a sudden downpour bashed down all around him. He was soaked, and ran for cover under a small overhang. As he did so, his feet clattered on the loose planks of a rickety wooden porch.

He stood in the darkness, shivering with cold. The poncho protected his torso, and he had its hood pulled up over the baseball cap. Still, his trouser legs were soaked, and water ran down his face.

He took out his phone and tried once again to get a signal, but the closest cell tower must be out.

At that moment, a woman's voice said, "Is someone out there?"

"I'm so sorry," Martin said. "My car died, and I had to run here to get out of the rain."

The front door opened a crack, and out peered a sturdy, youthful woman in a loose flowery shift. She had mussy dark hair, as if she'd been sleeping. Her face had a kind of horsy, athletic prettiness—no makeup—and the house emitted a sort of odd smell of kale and vegetarian fare marinated in strange spices. "Can you call for help?"

"My cell phone isn't connecting."

"Oh you poor thing. Well, come on inside and get dry. I have a fire going. You can warm up and use my landline."

"Thank you so much," Martin said as he stepped into the cottage and she rattled the locks shut on the door. She was older than he'd thought at first—kind of a hippie survivor with graying hair. She had a bandanna strapped around the top of her head. On second thought, she wasn't old enough to be a hippie, but more of a nostalgia fan. She had a solid, energetic body under that loose dress—probably a surfer.

That made him think again of Joe Logan. If only he could reach Joe, maybe someone at the Surf Board could pick him up. But how would he then get to LA?

"Can I get you some hot tea or something?" she asked. "My name is Marsha Starker."

"Martin Brown." He stripped off the poncho, which he let fall by the door, where it dripped onto a bristly doormat. He took off his soaked baseball cap and laid it on top as well. "Sorry. It's all wet."

"Don't worry. That's what the rug is for. Are you alone?"

"Yes. Heading to Los Angeles to see my girlfriend. Thank you so much for your kindness."

"What a night. We're at the start of a huge storm that is supposed to move east over the coast but it will go half the night."

"I was on my way up the street to call Uber. I did have a cell connection up there."

"It's sketchy down here at the beach," she said. "My partner Josie Klein is in the other room, building a dollhouse."

"Really." Martin was impressed at the odd hobbies people seemed to have.

"Oh yes," Marsha said. "Josie sells them for lots of money. It's how we can afford this expensive rental."

"I'm sorry to disturb you and Josie."

"Not at all." She raised her chin. "Josie, we have company!"

Martin did not hear a reply.

"She says welcome and make yourself at home. I'll get you some tea. Just have a seat there. You can look out the window at the storm."

Nice figure, Martin thought as Marsha hustled out of the living room and into a small kitchen just visible around the corner. The cottage was small. Its interior was wooden, with shiplath across the upper half, a beamed ceiling like a ski lodge, and two dangling ceiling lamps with soft amber electric bulbs glowing under tin shades. Bookshelves lined the walls, stuffed with a mix of collectibles, photos, paintings, and old hardcover print volumes. There was a large flagstone fireplace with black andirons and a brass grate. In a bucket stood steel tongs. On one side was a stack of split logs, on the other side a smaller stack of kindling wood.

A wooden counter with a few barstools set off the living room from the kitchen door. *Nice arrangement,* Martin thought.

A door led off to other parts of the house, including presumably the atelier or Josie's workshop. He wondered if he'd get a glimpse at the doll houses Josie was making. There had been a shop once in Old Town that sold dollhouses and miniatures. There must be a market for that, he thought.

Marsha stuck a pert, youthful face into the living room. "I like my tea with a shot of brandy. What about you?"

"Oh sure," Martin said. "That would be perfect on a night like this."

Marsha breezed through the living room. "I'll see if Josie wants to partake." She opened the door and disappeared into the hidden part of the house.

Martin overheard a conversation between two women—one in Marsha's robust voice, the other in a lighter, more melodious voice. That must be the dollhouse maker, Josie.

Martin absently fiddled with his phone while he waited. Still dead. He was about to ask if he could use the landline, but Marsha was busy. He caught sight of a different woman in a distant room. Josie wore a dark red dress, had reddish hair, and wore thick horn-rimmed glasses from what Martin could see in a glimpse.

Then Marsha was back, striding across the living room in her blue and green flowery shift with yellow blossoms on it. The door slipped shut behind her, cutting off Martin's view of the hallway and distant work room. "I'll have our tea in a moment. Then we'll call on the phone to get you some help."

"Much appreciated," he said. He felt kind of trapped, wishing he were on his way to LA, but he figured he must accept circumstances and be thankful.

"Here we are." Marsha came out of the kitchen at that same oddly rushed clip.

"No need to hurry on my account."

"I'm always like this," she said.

He noticed that she had a bit of an edge to her, a faint coldness mixed with anger. Must have had a bad day, he thought.

"I'm having a bit of trouble with the phone," she said. "The storm must be affecting the landlines as well."

Outside, thunder growled and lightning flashed in the rain-spattered window.

She brought two steaming mugs of tea, each with a paper square dangling on a string, and the tea bag still inside. "This will steep and be a good, strong brew for you. I like it with a little bite to it."

She set one cup down on the wooden counter. The stools were on the other side in the little walkway between kitchen and living room. "Here is yours." She paused opposite him, across the glass-topped coffee table strewn with magazines. *She must be putting brandy in*, Martin thought as he watched her pert behind hidden amid large cloth print flowers and leaves.

Having finished, she turned and set his tea before him.

She grabbed her tea form the counter and sat down opposite him, cradling the mug in both hands. "What do you do, Martin?"

"I'm a writer."

"Oh, how exciting. What do you write? Poetry? Stories?"

He grinned. "The Reasonably Good If Not So Great American Novel." He lifted his cup by its hot handle and sipped. "Delicious," he said. "Tastes a bit like peaches."

"It has peaches in it," she said appreciatively. "You are a man who knows his tea."

He sniffed. "Is that a little bit of almond in there as well?"

"Nuts," she said with a bright smile, showing her teeth as he rumpled her nose and cheeks up. "We are all a bit nuts, aren't we?"

He shrugged. For want of a rejoinder, he took another sip. It was hot, but sweet. He relished the comfort of the hot liquid. Warmth spread down his neck, his torso, and his limbs.

"I have stomach troubles," she said brightly. "Do you?" She rose and went into the kitchen. Moments later, she returned holding a bottle of clear liquid and a smaller brown bottle. "Angostura Bitters," she said. "I take some every day with club soda. Would you like some?"

My stomach is fine, he thought, but it seemed he could not speak.

She sat back down with that sunny expression on her face. She produced a clean glass from the bookshelf behind her, set it on the coffee table, and unscrewed the soda bottle lid. It made a loud hissing noise. Then it made a gurgling sound as she poured herself a full, fizzing glass. "I love this stuff," she said. "It is so soothing." She unscrewed the lid on the smaller bottle and shook it upside down over the glass. Reddish, bloody colored liquid fell into the club soda. The soda water became reddish-brown and glowed like a red lantern in the gloomy living room. It almost flickered hypnotically in the dancing light from the fireplace.

"I'll see if Josie wants to come join us," Marsha said.

Martin watched, paralyzed, as if he were sitting inside a fishtank looking out from the water.

"Josie!" Marsha called, turning toward the closed door. "Josie dear! Come on out and meet Mr. Martin Brown. He sneaked in here and thought he could fool us, but we fooled him, didn't we?" She gave Martin a look so filled with baleful hate and evil that he might have reacted with fear or a chill, except he felt numb all over. Waves upon waves of deadening neuropathy settled through his system. He could feel the drug—whatever she had given him—spreading along the axes, axons, and neurons, highways and byways, of his nervous system. So far, it was mostly clouding his peripheral nervous system, so that he could hardly lift a hand or twitch a finger. His legs felt as if they were made of rubber. It was not an altogether bad feeling, but rather pleasant, as if he was waiting to drift off to sleep.

As he started to realize too late that she had indeed fooled him, he began to notice signs of drug paraphernalia all around. She must be a medical tech or even a nurse. Under the couches and chairs were torn-open white or plastic bags with industrial-looking medical names on them. Syringes lay strewn about in the carpet. Pill bottles rolled around under the seats.

"Josie!" she called again, then popped up like a cork in a bathtub. "I'm going to tell her a thing or two." She whirled, in a spiral of flowery and leafy cotton, and rushed on shapely, strong legs toward the hallway door. Throwing it open, she strode away into the distance. She became a blur as Martin's eyes closed.

Hearing a yell, he tore his eyes open and saw that Josie had entered the room. She wore that long dark dress and the orange hair and heavy-rimmed glasses. But she must be Marsha's twin.

Martin blinked, trying to remain conscious and to make sense of these two women.

It was very hard, but he must try.

It was Marsha, wearing an orange wig and a dark gown. In fact, she wore the gown over her flowery dress. That was Marsha underneath the Josie get-up, stark raving mad.

And she carried a large butcher knife a foot long, with a chopping blade on it about three inches wide. The blade came to a point and curved upward in a razor sharp gutting hook.

Josie-Marsha plopped down opposite Martin. "You fucking guys!" she yelled. "You fucking guys! You fucking guys!" over and over again.

Martin sensed he was tipping to the right, ready to fall over. There was nothing he could do to steady himself, and she was not about to stop her tirade of hate and anger.

Marsh smiled brightly, "Josie is practicing her dance steps. Whoo-hooh!" With that she rose, and started to perform a kind of south Asian dance step with Balinese finger-pinching and Indian neck-twitching while blinking provocatively. She actually almost turned blue in the dim firelight.

Josie said, "You like that, eh, Martin? I am going to gut you like a fish."

No, he thought, *I have to get to see Chloë in LA.*

Josie danced ever more feverishly, while waving her knife around and making elegant pinching motions with the fingers of her opposite hand. Slowly, the orange wig toppled off, revealing Marsha's long, mussy graying hair underneath. As she danced, Marsha began using the knife to shred Josie's long dark red gown, as if trying to free Marsha from being Josie's prisoner.

In a hideous, grinding voice—a high-pitched witch's snarl— Marsha said, "As soon as I get Josie off me, Martin, I am going to lead you outside and feed you to the fishes of the sea. The storm is perfect because it will bring up the bottom feeders, who will feast on the pieces of you that I carve off for their lovely cuisine."

As she spoke, she waved the knife. It twirled around in a wide, twinkling circle, and caused a red gash to appear on her other arm. She shrieked and looked at blood pouring from a cut that ran across her forearm.

Screaming, she ran into the kitchen and could be heard opening and slamming drawers. "Bandages! Antibiotics!" she screamed. "I am bleeding. He did this to me, the bastard. Martin, you murdering bastard! You stabbed me."

As he listened, Martin kept tilting to the right until, finally, gravity took hold of him and he pitched face-down onto the coffee table. His face was just two or three feet from where she had sat. On a decorative wooden shelf above a lamp table sat the bottle of

Angostura Bitters. Beside it sat the half empty glass of reddish soda water mixed with bitters. That in itself was a totally normal, safe bartender's remedy for stomach upset. Next to it was an amber prescription bottle with its white lid off beside it. Squinting, Martin could make out the name of the drug she had slipped into his tea: *Xanax*.

Luckily he had only taken two or three sips of the hot tea and brandy with the drug mixed in, or he might be out cold.

With what little life was left in his arms and legs, he tried to push off, to stand up.

Instead, he fell sideways into the space between the coffee table and the couch where he had sat.

She was still screaming in the kitchen. He heard her throwing things, heard the crash of splintering glass as she pitched bottles and glasses about, and cups and saucers no doubt, working herself into a frenzy of madness.

He reclined with one cheek pressed against the filthy rug that had never been vacuumed. He lay helplessly, inhaling the smells of cat crap and muddy shoes, of spilled drinks and rotten food. There were huge dust balls under the couch. He wished he could crawl under the couch for safety, but his body wouldn't let him.

Distantly, the sound of her angry yelling could be heard rising to a shrieking climax, a ranting and raving crescendo.

There, directly ahead of him, lay a syringe. Next to it was a long white cardboard container with all sorts of cautionary labels. As nearly as he could make out, it was a dose of generic adrenaline—the kind used in operating rooms to poke directly into the heart of patients in cardiac arrest. It was a last resort, aside from defibrillating shocks, to try and get the heart pumping again. It was also mixed with Xylocain and Novocain in dentists' offices to speed the numbing drug through a patient's system.

Summoning all of his might, Martin inched his right hand up, one centimeter at a time, until his twitching, numb fingers closed on the syringe. He had lost almost all coordination, so his next maneuver would be hit or miss, live or die. With great effort, grunting, he turned the syringe around so that it faced him. Clutching his fist around it, he pulled it toward himself. Faster and faster it went, until he could feel a pricking sensation under his shoulder blade.

Immediately, he felt his numbness tempered with electric sparking sensations. His nervous system was fighting a war between

numbness and stimulation. He saw flashing lights. He felt his legs
and arms tremble as adrenaline surged through his blood stream.
With it came anger at this crazy woman or, more likely, at whoever
had let her loose from some institution for the dangerously insane.

In lurching motions, desperate jerking motions, Martin heaved
himself erect.

With Frankenstein movements, he rose up.

He fell down, making glasses crash somewhere nearby. He
hoped he was not cut.

Looking down, he saw that his thick hoodie must have deflected
shattered glass from a broken brandy snifter filled with green pothos
plant.

He lurched from one support to another, heading toward the
door.

As he went, he could hear speaking on the phone. "...He tried
to murder me and my sister. This bastard! I let him in out of the rain,
and he took out a huge butcher knife. What's that? Yes, I got his
name. It's Angus Stura Bitters. He is about five eleven, in his early
twenties, with short brown hair and brown eyes. He is extremely
dangerous. I think he is still in the house, and he is trying to kill
me...What's that? Marsha Starker..."

As she spelled out her name, Martin staggered to the front door.
It was like swimming through dark water. He felt pulled in many
directions between the influence of the numbing drug and the
electrical jolt of the adrenaline.

"You fucking bastard!" she screamed as she craned her neck
and poked her head from the kitchen into the living room. She saw
him and dropped the receiver.

With a wild animal shriek, she raised the butcher knife and
launched herself at him in a tangle of flowery garment.

Martin felt his stamina returning.

As she reached him, he sidestepped her.

She crashed loudly against the front door and fell onto his piled
poncho.

Martin ran as best he could toward the glass sliding door
overlooking the back of the house. Tearing it open, he staggered out
into a wild, sleeting rain.

Lightning flashed.

In the revelations of light, he saw that he was on a small,
poured-concrete back porch.

If only he could make it away from here!

He began to run across the wet sand.

His shoes, already wet, became soaked as he stepped into one deep puddle after another.

The cold water seemed to snap him out of his narcotic haze.

He focused on pumping his arms and putting one foot in front of the other as he ran toward the sea.

Thunder slammed and ricocheted around him.

Each time lightning flashed, he could gain some instant flicker of recognition—he was on a beach, looking at a roiling sea with ten foot walls of seething, blasting, exploding foam. Rain flew sideways in the strong, icy wind.

Behind him, he heard a scream as Marsha launched herself after him.

Flying from the porch, screaming and screeching at top volume, she waved the knife in the air and ran after him.

She was faster than he was in his lumbering state.

He ran as best he could.

No time to even glance over his shoulder.

He could hear her breath sawing over his shoulder.

He glimpsed her wide, frantic eyes.

Her pupils were little black dots in the middle of huge white eyeballs.

Her mouth was wide open, with little purple lips stretched to their maximum, revealing a heap of blue tongue and the black around her tonsils as she alternately breathed in and screamed out.

As she ran, she made repeated attempts to slash him with the knife.

Between a combination of his dodging and her incoherent motions, she missed two or three times.

Each of those powerful slashing blows could have severely wounded or killed him.

He cried out in terror as his voice returned.

Finally, he realized he had lost.

He was about to die.

He turned, and staggered backward, looking his killer directly in her animal eyes.

Marsha might as well be airborne, given the fluttering of her soaked gown in the lashing rain.

Lightning flashed, flashed, flashed.

Her facial features had become a grimacing mask from hell.

As he backed away, rapidly losing ground, he fell over backward and landed heavily on his rump. The fall stunned him.

He watched as she came toward him.

But she too stumbled on the buried brick fire pit that had made him fall.

With one last scream, she aimed the knife at his heart.

But she fell, and landed on the knife.

Martin was in the act of pulling himself away, crawling to put distance between himself and her.

A moment later, there was only lightning, and lashing rain, and howling wind.

She lay dead on her back, with the knife sticking from her chest.

Lightning flashed again, just an instant, too brief to make out any facial expression. He only glimpsed a gray death mask staring away into eternity.

Sobbing in spiritual exhaustion, Martin heaved himself to his feet.

He staggered away to find his car.

Behind him, he heard the door of another house crashing open and shut. He heard voices and running feet. He heard a woman screaming, "There is a woman dead on the sand! She's been stabbed through the heart."

A man yelled, "Honey, get in here quick. I'll call the cops. There is an insane murderer on the loose out here."

"We'll be next," the woman wailed. She must have run back to the house, because a door slammed and there was silence.

Martin ran and stumbled around the house, never wanting to set foot inside again.

The car was where he had left it.

He got in and tried the ignition. It labored and labored but would not turn over.

He thought about breaking into the house and calling police.

At that moment, through the waves and sheets of blowing wind and rain, he saw flashing blue and red lights passing on the street above, right by the corner where the car had finally died.

The police were already there.

He jogged up the sidewalk, feeling his strength and presence of mind returning. He would be saved now. The nightmare would be over in a few minutes.

He reached the top of the street, just in time for a speeding patrol car with flashing lights to streak past. He overheard a radio voice saying, "All cars, be on the lookout for a male age twenty-two, with short brown hair, going by the name of Angus Story or Stury Bitters. Just got a report of a stabbing victim dead on the beach. Suspect is armed and highly dangerous...."

Martin thought about turning himself in and ending this. He was the suspect. He was Angus Story Bitters, crazed killer, or however this insane woman in her madness and viciousness had tried to frame him. But he had a right not to be implicated in something that might cost him thirty years to life if it came to a court case and sanity lost. Or the other side had a better lawyer. What if she had a rich family who could hire one of those television lawyers? He was innocent. Let them sort things out. He must get away. He had done nothing wrong. All he wanted to do was reach Chloë. It was all he cared about. And when Martin made up his mind to do something, only hell itself would stop him. He was one of those unstoppable Alienopolis heroes with the fluttering cape. Hadn't Chloë described him that way? He must escape from this hell and get to LA.

Chapter 6. Jimmy Sprocket

Homeless, hopeless—as he walked in the rain, Martin was less conscious of being hunched over, shivering, and wet than he was of having witnessed what amounted to a madwoman's suicide, or maybe legally self-manslaughter, or make that womanslaughter. She had tried to murder him, and had killed herself instead. None of it was his fault—yet every fiber in his being, from a lifetime of principle and well-meaning, demanded that he turn himself in and explain the truth. At the same time, he kept calculating that he might be mistakenly presumed to have murdered the woman, or some other crime. All he had done was step briefly on a porch to get out of the rain after his car broke down. Now he just wanted to reach Los Angeles, cuddle with Chloë, and make a try at working for Alienopolis—which would be the dream of a lifetime.

He was now without a car—which sat outside the dead woman's house—so it would not be long before he was at least circumstantially connected with the case by police. There would be fingerprints inside the house. Yes, he was more tempted than ever to flag down one of those cruisers with flashing lights passing in the rain. But he wasn't ready—not yet. His momentum and stubbornness pointed toward LA. So he resolved to keep trudging until he got things properly mulled over in his head. He had over two hundred dollars in his wallet, so he would have enough to eat and something to treat Chloë to sushi.

Rain continued beating down. Lightning flashed, and thunder growled.

Martin sought refuge in a glassed-in bus shelter. There, as if by a miracle, he found an old army-type blanket folded neatly on one of four benches arranged in a C-shape. Gratefully, he draped himself in the blanket, smelling a combination of horse manure and machine oil. If he had to guess, he thought the blanket might have fallen from one of those trailers transporting a horse—maybe to or from the Del Mar Fair Grounds not far south, in fact not far from where Joe Logan was just now tending bar.

Martin looked at his cell phone, which still had juice, though the battery indicator was down one bar. It was now eight p.m. He had been on the road barely three hours, and already his world had forever changed. Worse yet, he would have been at the UCLA campus by now had the automobile gods cooperated. How was it possible that fate could throw such boomerangs at his head?

He thought about calling Joe. What would that accomplish? He might get ride home in the wee hours of the morning. Bars closed by two a.m., and staff normally worked at least an hour or two cleaning up, setting up, counting money, and so forth to close out one day and prepare for a six a.m. opening. Poor Chloë—

what must she be thinking? She was probably getting worried.

He stared at the phone. Should he call? Would he sound normal? Or would he sound so weird and depressed that she would become frightened. He resolved to call her—but to wait a little while first, to calm down, consider his options.

At the moment, he was wet and cold. The army blanket was by now a warm, soggy wrapper. It kept out the worst of the wind. Oh god it was hailing now. What else? Hail the size of meatballs rattled down on the street, banging on the roofs of cars parked along the curb. Not only that, but the hail balls bounced around. The wind drove them in little herds, in circles, in rows spinning down the street. Water rushed in gutters, carrying anything past that wasn't nailed down. Martin watched a brick, a newspaper, a child's doll, a garden gnome still holding its lantern, and an empty gallon wine bottle go sailing past.

The nuclear option occurred to him. He could make the ultimate surrender and call his parents. His dad would not hesitate to brave the elements, possibly with a leering, triumphant Nancy perched in the passenger seat to lecture him on why he was the most stupid male for miles around; after hugging him, of course. Ee-yeahhh.... Maybe not, after about two seconds' contemplation. What about Alicia or Joe or anyone else? He decided to consider the Joe option after midnight. Joe was just down the road a few miles. He could swing by and pick Martin up if worst came to worst. Then again, how much more worst could worst become? Okay, he made up his mind, he'd call Joe at eleven. Barring that, he'd call Uber and get a ride home. He'd have to explain to Chloë that fate had intervened. His heart was broken.

Right about that moment, he saw a very strange sight.

Coming down the street was a young man on a bicycle, driving in this storm. The guy was hunched over, pumping the pedals with trudging, laborious slowness while gripping the handle bars. It was an older model bicycle, not quite a clunker, but not a racing bike. It was maybe what marketing people called a touring bike. The guy riding it had a hat pulled over his features, just revealing a hard-bitten face and a frontiersman's beard. He was draped with a black poncho whose shiny wet rubber surfaces kept getting clobbered—*plop, plop*—with hail. On his back, the bicyclist carried a huge rucksack with all sorts of appendages hanging from it, including ragged, folded garbage bags—the entire *Gestalt* bespoke homelessness and a kind of tidy desperation.

The fellow slid off his bike and wheeled it into the bus stop. "Evening."

"Hi," Martin said. "Out for a spin?"

"Not by choice." The man was a few years older than Martin, and might have been even older, so weather-beaten were his features. The beard made him look even older. He had not had a haircut in a long time, but tied his dirty-looking, stringy locks back into a ponytail. "What a night."

"You're telling me." Martin sat wrapped in the blanket, certain he looked even more miserable than he felt.

"What's your story?"

"You first."

"Not much to tell. I had a life once. That's years ago. Now I live where I can—sometimes beside the freeway, other times by the river down in San Diego. I sell cans, do odd jobs, get laid when I can, smoke dope when I can, get drunk whenever possible. I think that about covers it."

"I had a life," Martin said. "Up until about three hours ago. My car died, and I think I died not long after."

"Bummer," said the man. "I'm Jim. Call me Jimmy. No last name. Gave up on that when I became homeless. Folks sometimes call me Sprocket because of the bicycle."

"Looks like a nice bicycle."

"I didn't steal it, if that's your next question." Jimmy was a tall, skinny man with sunken cheeks and bitter blue eyes. After pulling the bike out of the rain, he dug around in one of the backpack's many pockets until he found some tobacco, papers, and a lighter. It took him all of thirty seconds to roll a cigarette that looked like a joint, lick each end, and prop it between clenched teeth. The lighter flickered into life on the third click, and he inhaled. "You want?"

"Don't smoke, but thanks."

"The guy who owned that bike left it to me when he died of cancer. He went into the Veterans' Hospital in La Jolla and never came out. It was lung cancer. He was about sixty, I think. Jerry Montana. People called him that because he was from Montana. Nice guy."

"Sad story."

"Suits the evening. Where are you headed?"

"Los Angeles."

"Why?"

"Chick."

"I getcha. Noblest of causes. Or dumbest, if you're being had."

"Right."

"Right what? You're being had, or being noble?"

Martin laughed. "I feel noble, but then if I were being had, how would I know?"

Jimmy nodded as he sucked on his cigarette and filled the station with acrid smoke, like a burning bus or something. Martin coughed and waved a hand over his face. Jimmy shrugged. "You got any food? Dope? Anything to trade?"

"Just the blanket on my back."

Jimmy eyed the blanket with mercenary precision. "Looks like a good one. You keep it."

"It's all I got," Martin said.

"That and a chick in LA and a ton of hope. Man, I envy you."

Seizing the moment, Martin said, "Look, I don't have any experience at this. How would you get to LA if you were in my shoes?"

"Hitch, probably. I'd wait until it's not monsoon season though. You learn to be patient. Worst comes to worst, you just go to sleep somewhere under cover until it's over. Assuming you're in a safe place. Me, I stay away from other homeless people unless I absolutely got to go near them for however long I need to and not a second more."

"Don't trust them, eh?"

Jimmy laughed, showing a row of missing or brown and rotten teeth. "You trust people?"

"I have my friends from school. My family. What about you?"

He shrugged. "I was put outside at an early age. My dad did drugs and beat us. My mom turned tricks she said to support us but ended up in a crack-snorting rodeo. They were both dead by the time I was fifteen."

"Any brothers and sisters?"

He shook his head. From his expression, Martin could see that Jimmy was beyond bitterness. He had accepted his fate. "My oldest brother used to molest my sisters. We finally beat him to within an inch of his life." He suddenly looked at Martin with big, haunted, otherworldly eyes. "You don't want to hear this. I relive it whenever I tell about it or think about it."

Martin fell silent. He was suffering from the cold. He shivered like an abandoned dog. The shivering came from the bones deep down. His entire body and soul trembled.

"Come on, man. We need to get us some hot grub. You with me?" Jimmy rose and prepared his bicycle home on wheels for the next little journey. "You come with me, you'll stop shivering."

"O-o-o-k-k-k-ay-ay-ay," Martin shivered.

Lightning flashed, and artillery boomed as the two figures trudged in a gray, seething rain. The hail had stopped, but cold glassy fibers of rain filled the air. The wind had died down, so the water fell straight down as from a million faucets.

Jimmy walked his bicycle with the big backpack tied to its seat like an inanimate passenger.

Martin walked beside him with the blanket draped over his head—heavy and soaked, but shielding him from the constant battery of water. Beside him, Jimmy looked like a man in a shower with rain runneling from his long hair and beard. When Jimmy talked, rainwater fell from his mustache.

Occasional squad cars raced by on a mission to find the Beach Killer.

Jimmy had a little radio on which he played rock music; he kept it in a plastic sandwich baggie hanging from the handlebars by a twist of old-fashioned coat hanger.

"Man, you know anything about that?"

Martin shook his head.

"You said your name is Martin?"

Martin nodded.

Jimmy looked at him with big, scared, haunted eyes that had seen horror before. "You ain't Angus Story Bitters, are you?"

"Never heard of the man," Martin said.

After a half hour the two soggy, wading allies arrived at a little wooden building at the edge of a eucalyptus grove. A neon cross hovered over the white shingled walls. Through an open, ogive-shaped, double door up a flight of steps, Martin could hear singing. An organ played, and people clapped powerfully in rhythm.

Jimmy Sprocket put a hand out against Martin's chest. "We can dry our clothes and get a bite to eat. But first you gotta spend an hour singing and praying."

"What denomination are they?"

Jimmy shook his head. "Does it matter? They're all crazy. They believe in imaginary beings and ghosts."

"Don't you?"

Jimmy flashed a slit of brown teeth. "I'm a survivor, man. You feed me, I will pray to anyone or anything you worship. Be it rocks, trees, or dead people. I seen it all."

They made their way up the steps. The vestibule was clean and well lighted. A large blond-haired, crew-cut man who could be a former boxer greeted them. He wore a black suit and introduced himself as Deacon Gabriel Ramirez. "Bless the Lord, brothers. Welcome to His sanctuary."

"Amen," said Jimmy.

"Amen," echoed Martin.

"Bless the Lord," Deacon Ramirez repeated. With large, powerful hands, he removed the sodden blanket and ushered Martin into a side room that smelled of cloth and lye. Stacks of freshly laundered clothing stood about. An ethnically diverse mix of men and women in simple but clean clothing sorted and folded clothing. Two black women wearing red dresses—one with a large yellow hat, the other a large blue hat—ironed on two boards that gave off a pleasant smell of hot linen tinged with ammonia.

Deacon Ramirez intoned, "We clean the body, we clean the soul. We nourish the belly, we feed the faith. Welcome to Al-Balaam, savior of the galaxy."

"What?" Martin asked in a tiny, scared voice.

"Don't worry," Jimmy said. "You're probably from some standard, stay-pressed church. I don't ask, you don't tell. It don't matter when you are shivering and hungry. These guys have been around for a long time."

"Who is Al-Balaam?"

"Who is Alienopolis?"

"You know about Alienopolis?" Martin said, suddenly impressed.

"Who hasn't heard of Alienopolis?" Jimmy said as he started to peel off his outer layers of soiled clothing. "I may be working for them soon."

"Building strange new worlds," Jimmy said. "You go guy."

Now that they were in a dry building with standard yellowish electric lighting, Martin could see that Jimmy literally wore rags. He wore multiple sweaters that fit him like sheets of fungus, with holes literally rotting off of him. Underneath were yellowish, stained layers of T-shirts whose predominant shades were yellow and gray in overlapping cloud-patterns.

"Been a while, brother," said Deacon Ramirez as he held up a plastic trash bag for Jimmy to deposit his clothing. "Showers are in the side by the sanctuary. You guys go get cleaned up, put on some fresh clothes, and join us to sing hymns of praise."

"Amen, brother," said Jimmy with a distant layer of sarcasm masked by an intense show of faith and humility.

Martin found himself trembling with joy just to be dry and warm again. His body had become a shipwreck of shivering timbers, sailing unknown seas in a storm, or something like that. He was beyond poetry and metaphor. This was reality, or something approximating it.

Whatever happened to his clothes, he made sure he kept his wallet close and tight. It had his I.D. cards, driver's license, credit cards, and cash—several hundred semoleans, intended to impress Chloë.

"You are welcome to join the Holy Sanctuary Church of Al-Balaam and rejoice in the Spirit of Salvation," Deacon Ramirez intoned. "Al-Balaam is the Prophet of God. Rejoice!"

The rocking and singing in the church continued unabated while Jimmy and Martin shed their wet clothing and now wore white sheets.

"These are the white garments of the elect," intoned Deacon

Ramirez .

He was joined by an equally large black man in a black suit. "I am Deacon Greg Beor," said the newcomer. "I will help ready you for the Lord. Follow me."

Martin and Jimmy left their clothes behind in soggy piles on the floor. Women in the sanctuary rushed in to scoop the clothing up in trash bags. "We will clean them and return them to you so that your garments will be purified," so sayeth Deacon Beor. "A warm shower with lots of soap and water will be your next *odor* of business."

Martin rejoiced in the warmth. His shivering body slowly unclenched. His muscles ached where they had been cold and tight. He and Jimmy stood under separate shower heads, masked in a thick cloud of hot steam.

"This is wonderful," Martin said. "I have never enjoyed a shower so much."

In fact, just getting warm was painful when he'd been cold and wet for at least an hour.

"You are sincere," Jimmy said. "They will like that."

"Who are these people?"

Jimmy shrugged. "The world is full of mysteries. You people who whizz by in the cars and have jobs, you go to college and cash paychecks, you own dogs and cats that you do not eat to survive— you have no idea what goes on in reality, right under your noses."

"Wow," Martin said. "We are inside the bizarre worlds of Alienopolis."

"Amen, brother."

"You weren't talking like that a few minutes ago," Martin said while sudsing himself with a large lilac-scented bar of department store soap.

"We adapt to fit the occasion," Jimmy said. "It's evolution. We are chameleons. We change our spots as necessary. That's how I have stayed alive all these years. I beat the demon dope that killed my parents."

"You do smoke marijuana," Martin suggested. "You were asking about dope when we first met."

"Oh that, yeah." Jimmy scrubbed his underarms with a washcloth, keeping one arm half raised. "Some of these churches use Mary Jane as a sacrament. The key is to let nothing surprise you."

Martin nodded. "This is heaven."

"They believe it is the doorway to heaven."

"And this is sunny Southern California."

"It never rains in Southern California," Jimmy ad-libed tunelessly from a long-ago rock song. "But when it rains, oh Lord it pours, man it pours…I wanna go ho-o-o-o-o-m-m-e…"

Martin could have cried, thinking about how he missed the sunshine on the beach by the crab shack. He longed to be with his buddies—Paul Lo, Joe Logan, Harry Markowitz, Rob Castillo—and the women of their gang—Alicia Washington, Carol Monegan— with all of their secrets and whatnots. So according to Maritza Dusenbery, old quiet blonde bland Carol Monegan had a secret second life as a woman-loving superheroine. What else?

"We only live once," Jimmy Sprocket said amid puffs of steam. He raised his face as if rejoicing in the Lord, or in the hot water deliciously pummeling him. "Enjoy our passage through this vale of tears and terrors, and make the most of every opportunity for three hots and a cot."

"I think I am developing prune skin," Martin said, looking at bluish-white fingertips that resembled decaying grapes.

"Time to get out and start praying. My stomach is growling up a thunderstorm." Jimmy reached up with a bare, brown arm and turned off a large industrial faucet.

Martin did the same.

"Grab a towel and rejoice," Jimmy said. As they briskly toweled in a locker room nearby, whose tiles smelled of hot chlorine, he added, "They like it when you rejoice a lot."

"I'm rejoicing," Martin said.

"You sound sincere," Jimmy said admiringly.

"I am sincere. This hot shower has been one of the happiest moments of my life."

"We are salvaged."

"We are saved."

"That too. Keep rejoicing, brother."

"Amen," Martin said.

"Get that singing voice tuned up," Jimmy urged darkly.

The main hall of the church rocked with music and singing, clapping and tambourines. Men and women in nice clothing clapped and rocked in rhythm. Some of the hymns sounded familiar to Martin, while others seemed other-worldly.

Martin had eaten dinner in late afternoon at the diner, where he'd spoken with Chloë. That seemed like worlds away now. He rocked and clapped—why not? It was fun and kept you moving.

About a hundred late-night worshipers crowded the church. It resembled any radically Puritanic house of worship—no stained glass, no altar, nothing to recall the hated popery and potpourri.

Seeing the look on Martin's face, Jimmy Sprocket nudged him and whispered, "Everyone thinks they have the only true magic." His voice took on a mocking tone, even as a whisper, "My magic is stronger than your magic. I have to kill you because your magic is evil and mine is the only correct magic. What a bunch of fucking assholes."

Martin felt horrified and made a shush-finger over his mouth. "You'll get us thrown out. We want to have lunch, remember?"

"I must be delirious."

"You studied philosophy."

"I am a dropout. It's an ugly episode ten years ago. I never discuss it."

"Where?"

"Harvard."

"Oh my god."

"Yeah. My I.Q. is like a Boeing plane type. My lifestyle is like a total plane crash."

"You're doing the best you can."

"Thank you for understanding."

They clapped and swayed with the best of them. The parishioners were a mix of every race and color on earth, about equally male and female. No children were present.

"Rock of Ages, Sock my Pages, Dock my Wages," Jimmy sang loudly by Martin's side. Only Martin could hear his bastardized lyrics. "Crock of Sages, Mock my Cages," Jimmy warbled while the thundering rhythmic yelling of the congregation and their clapping and foot stomping drowned out his heresies. "Clock my Phages, Rock my Mages, Flock my Rages," Jimmy muttered into Martin's ear.

At some point, the drummer rocked a roll and the guitarist miffled a riff. People cheered and waved fists. "Glory be to Al-Balaam, Savior of the Universe."

The Reverend Damual Shultz rose to the podium. "Brothers and Sisters!" He was a big black man with short kinky hair, skin the color of cocoa butter, and a thousand-dollar suit under his purple cassock.

"Oh yeah!" intoned the choir. The organ wheedled and toodled. "Reverend!" and "Right On!" and "Al-Balaam!"

"Brothers and Sisters," croaked Reverent Shultz. He wiped his lips with a white handkerchief big enough to be a dinner napkin. "Every day, every week, all year long, we sing and pray the glory of our Savior, Al-Balaam. Now if you want to see proof of His great works, look into the gardens and the vineyards where penitents toil. We have a well-oiled machinery that operates on the industrial skyline with the best and latest spiritual technologies."

"Amen!" the crowd intoned.

A woman fainted, and two men carried her to the back.

The organ made an ice skating or baseball half time *whoo-whoo* sound.

"Oh yeah!" a row of sturdy men chanted together, rocking left and right while clapping big work-worn hands. All wore expensive suits.

Reverend Shultz spread his arms as if embracing the world. He half shouted, half sang in a preacher's voice, "We thank you, Al-Balaam, Lord of the Universe. You sanctify our works, which are made to praise your holy name."

Your woolly game, Jimmy whispered quietly, and Martin cringed. Jimmy did live dangerously.

"The gardens of Al-Balaam are filled with repentance. Penitents till Our Lord's vineyards and labor in his groves. Wealth flows through our hands to glorify the Lord God of the Universe. Hallelujah!"

The rapes of wrath, the grapes of wealth, Jimmy almost telepathed.

"You, Sir!" Reverend Shultz raged, suddenly pointing at Jimmy with a large finger. "You, Sir, must repent! You are new here."

"Amen," Jimmy said loudly. He raised his hands at the sky while waving his arms like underwater seaweed. He nudged Martin sharply with one hip. "You too, asshole."

"You Sir!" Reverend Shultz bellowed, aiming that bazooka finger at Martin.

"Hallelujah!" Martin wailed loudly and waved his arms. In his mind, he added, *Now they screw ya.* He was taking a page from Jimmy's book.

The organ pulsed out a note that kept going and rose higher and higher, taking tension to the heavens. "My friends, we are here to pray with these newcomers that they will be saved by the Lord Al-Balaam's grace and love. It's not a free ride. We have to pitch in, till the earth, prune the vines, graft the blossoms that rise on high."

Martin began to fade a bit. The preacher's yelling was like rap music, beating on his ears with doggerel rhyme, full of sound and fury, signifying whatever.

Then it was over. Mercifully, the sermon came to an end.

The worship continued, but an usher—a woman in a pink dress—walked down the aisle, picking the homeless and hopeless who had prayed enough and were now due for some lunch.

With an exchange of looks, Jimmy and Martin sidled out of their pew and walked up a carpeted ramp to the rear of the church. There, besides showers, reception, and other services posted by name over their respective doorways, was the Kitchen.

Already, a line of scraggly looking newly-washeds stood waiting their turn to pick up a tray, cafeteria style, then plates and silverware, and walk past a chow line.

Martin felt a sense of panic growing. He wasn't particularly hungry, having eaten earlier. A light snack might do. The hot cocoa looked appealing after his ordeal. He told Jimmy, "I'm trying to get to LA. Otherwise, I might as well take an Uber and go home."

Jimmy whispered back, "Maybe these people can get you there. Go ask. It's only a two-hour drive, right?"

"That's what I thought four hours ago." Nevertheless, Martin did wander out of line and into the lobby, where he spotted Deacon Greg Beor. The huge, ex-football-player-looking man in expensive charcoal suit stood with his hands modestly folded, giving directions to various groups of parishioners who came with questions or filed in and out of the worship service.

"Yes? Mr.?"

"Martin Brown, Sir. I am in desperate need of help."

Deacon Beor's features wrinkled sympathetically. "What is it, my son?"

Martin explained as briefly as possible about his need to get to Los Angeles.

Deacon Beor nodded understandingly. His eyes maintained a veiled, thoughtful look. "Maybe something can be arranged."

"Could you get me to LA tonight? Is there someone from among these many people heading there by any chance?"

"The Lord works in strange ways," Deacon Beor said.

Martin felt his stomach knot with desire for Chloë and anxiety about missing out on the biggest change of his life. "Yes?"

"Sometimes the direct way is not always the Lord's choice." The Deacon regarded Martin to see if Martin had understood his deep thought. "Sometimes the Lord Al-Balaam chooses a zig-zag path for us."

"Like my ending up here after my car broke down?" He didn't mention the storm, or the dead woman.

Deacon Beor made a cryptic face and shrugged. "You might say that, and more."

"Can you help me?"

"We can always help you. Helping you, we help ourselves."

"I'll be glad to wait here if you can ask around."

"Oh no, it's a done deal. We can get you where you need to go. There is a vehicle leaving in the next twenty minutes. You are just in time."

"Thank you, thank you!" Martin tried to pump the Deacon's hand.

Beor held back. "Thank the Lord Balaam. We are simply His tools in this world."

Martin went to find Jimmy, who was just then dining on a huge plate of fried chicken, mashed potatoes and gravy, peas and carrots, and an apple cobbler for dessert.

Martin told him the news.

"Hey, that's wonderful," Jimmy said. "Good luck, brother."

Martin stuck out a hand. "Thanks for everything."

"Think nothing of it." Jimmy returned an oddly limp shake, with a strange look to one side.

With nothing more to say, Martin walked back into the main lobby.

What did he need to do before boarding that ride to LA? He patted himself down. *My wallet*—ah, he felt its reassuring fatness on his left buttock. Great. Whatever else he might have taken along was in the trunk of his car in front of the late Marsha Starker's home.

Barely ten minutes later, Deacon Beor gave him the high sign. "Outside in the parking lot," he mouthed, pointing out the front door.

Martin almost had tears of joy and gratitude in his eyes when he saw a clean white bus with the legend Holy Sanctuary Church of Al-Balaam in black lettering above the front windshield.

He walked outside and examined the bus. It resembled one of those airport jitneys—not quite a big bus, but more than a van or an SUV.

A pleasant (or amused) looking middle-aged black man in a chauffeur's uniform (black suit, white shirt, black string tie) stood by the accordion door over the jitney step. "Will you be riding with us, sir?"

"Yes. Going north to LA."

"Oh? That's nice." The driver made a sweeping motion with both hands, pointing up the step. "Be my guest. You're the first person on board tonight."

"Thank you so much." Eagerly, Martin climbed up the two steps and found himself standing on clean black rubber flooring. Standing by the driver's cockpit, he looked into the bus and saw it had several rows of forward-facing benches in back. There were luggage racks overhead. Below that on each side was a long bench seat cased in pleasant-looking red plastic material.

"Pick a seat," the driver said. "The others will be joining you in a minute or two."

Martin wandered down the aisle under moderate lighting and picked a seat in the first row facing the front.

Two or three minutes later, a cheer arose from the vestibule of the church as a knot of about twenty parishioners came out dancing, singing, clapping their hands above their heads. Some of them gyrated in the parking lot. Others carried suitcases and military-style duffel bags out. A throng in the parking lot cheered, forming a corridor that the travelers passed through on their way to the bus.

Martin was tired, and thrilled to be on his way again. He took out his cell phone and finally had the courage to call Chloë. She answered on the third ring. "Martin?"

"Hi, Chloë. It's me."

"I've been worried about you. I thought you would be here by now."

"I'm sorry, sweetheart. It's been something of an ordeal. My car broke down and I was caught in that rainstorm."

"Oh you poor darling. I saw it on the TV news. They said San Diego got hit pretty hard. You have snow in the mountains at 3,000 feet."

"I believe it. Well, I'm just sitting in a bus now, and I should be on my way any minute. I can't wait to see you."

"I can't wait to see you either. What's that noise?"

Just then, about twenty chanting, clapping celebrants boarded the bus, which rocked under their weight.

"I can't hear you," said Chloë distantly.

"I can't wait to see you," he said, but the noise was too much.

Men and women—black, white, Hispanic, Asian, and other—talked excitedly as they stashed their luggage overhead.

They all took seats, and the bus driver—the middle-aged man in chauffeur uniform—climbed on board. Facing the crowd, he said, "Are we all on board and ready to go?"

"Oh yes," said a chorus, while clapping.

"All right," he said, "Then let's be on our way."

With that, he reached to one side and pulled a prison-like grating shut. It slid across the floor with a metallic grinding noise and clanged shut with a sense of finality.

Martin's joy dissolved in panic, then terror.

The rear door of the bus opened, and in climbed three or four Deacon types, all giant men wearing suits and black leather gloves. They looked like they meant business. Deacon Gabriel Ramirez and Deacon Greg Beor were among them. Two of them went down the bus, pulling shades down over the windows so the people inside could not see out, and anyone outside could not see inside.

Martin heard the rattle of chains, and saw with horror that the deacons were running chains across the seats. One by one, they handcuffed the parishioners to the chains, which were anchored in hand rails above each seat. Most people willingly raised their hands, allowing themselves to be cuffed.

Martin struggled to rise, but two of the giant men pressed him down in his seat.

The last thing he saw of the outside world was the sight of Jimmy Sprocket on his bicycle, accepting a gift of money from Reverend Damual Shultz. Jimmy Sprocket pedaled away into the drizzly night as fast as he could.

Martin felt like crying. "No, no, no," he sobbed as handcuffs gripped his wrists harshly and painfully. "What is this? Where are we going?"

The deacons laughed and took seats, two at either end of the prison van.

A skinny young blonde woman with crazed blue eyes told Martin, "We are going to labor in the vineyards of the Lord Al-Balaam. Didn't you hear the reverend give his sermon? We are going to do penance to save our souls and to save the world."

"This is fucking nuts," Martin wailed.

"Hush, dear, you have a filthy mouth," said a middle-aged Filipina.

"Oh god," Martin cried out. "Oh god please help me."

An India or Pakistani looking youth of about twenty nodded, "The Lord Al-Balaam is helping us all. You just don't know it yet."

"Surrender," cried a fervent, Mexican-looking man. "Give your soul to the Lord, and work in the fields."

The Filipina woman leaned forward and said confidentially, "Don't worry, dear, it is hard labor but bracing. If you get to till the marijuana plantations, you'll be high all the time. If you work in the vineyards, they let you drink wine to keep your spirits up." She laughed, as if the last statement was a joke.

Martin fell silent in stunned horror as the next chapter of his saga unfolded.

A serious older man explained, "You caught the part about the industrial skyline and all that. The Lord Al-Balaam has anointed certain people, including Chinese and Indian billionaires, to lead the world into a new age of peace and freedom. No more world wars or oil wars. It's a new Gilded Age of corporate peace and glory. We have the privilege to be a new kind of front-line soldier. We don't kill—we till. We don't die—we fly. We don't suffer—we buffer."

The Filipina lady nodded. "It's all for the good. You'll see."

Chapter 7. Take Me For A Ride

Sobbing, Martin Brown sat aboard the bus as it hove through the night. The lights were dimmed, and Deacon Ramirez announced, "Better get some sleep because we'll start working in the Lord's fields and vineyards the minute we arrive. It won't be long, because we are going to fly."

Ohhh... came a chorus of wonder and delight.

Martin shook his head, barely able to see through teary eyes. People around him sang and clapped. Their manacles added snap to the rhythm of their fervor.

In less than an hour, the bus slowed down and began making winding motions. Martin could not see outside because of the dark shades, but the bus was now traveling very slowly and making numerous left and right turns.

"Palomar Airport," Deacon Beor announced with satisfaction. "Reverend Shultz and the Shanghai Corporation have arranged for our jitney to be lifted onto a cargo plane for efficiency, and flown out to our own airport just north of the Salton Sea. The Lord Al-Balaam's people own several thousand acres, where we perform our penances with joy and hope. Uplift your souls in charity and love, because you may be sacrificing years of your life, but you will gain a window seat on the eternal journey to follow."

"Years?" Martin echoed in a whisper.

The Indian man nodded. "I signed up to spend the rest of my natural life working for the Lord. How about you?"

Martin shook his head and cried softly. "No, no, no…"

The servants and ministers of Lord Al-Balaam were not wasting any time. Evidently, cargo in the form of marijuana and wine barrels came in on one or more cargo flights. Martin heard a whisper that they would be carried in a converted, obsolete Boeing 707—retired and sold from the world's commercial air fleets decades ago.

As he felt giant cranes lift the bus into the air and swing it through the cargo hatch of the plane, Martin tearfully remembered the sight of Jimmy Sprocket accepting money from Reverend Shultz. So Jimmy had sold him for money. What a pal. What a rotten, devious son of a bitch. Martin felt a mix of rage, hate, and revulsion toward the smelly bearded creature with those rotten teeth.

The bus swung through the air and was gently placed on the

steel cargo floor. Martin twisted and fumbled but could not gain any freedom—he was tightly chained along with the others.

He heard the rattle of chains as the bus was fastened down on the cargo deck where long ago there had been seats for passengers.

Soon, the aircraft engines began to whine louder and louder as the craft rolled down the runway.

Martin had been to Palomar Airport to fly or to pick up friends, and he could picture the scene outside. The 707 was rolling along faster and faster with its engines laboring. In a few minutes, its pitch changed as the wheels separated from the runway and the plane nosed up toward heaven and the Lord Al-Balaam.

Just as quickly, its trajectory formed an arc as it topped off at probably 5,000 feet, cruised for a few minutes, and began its descent. It would deliver nearly two dozen new slave laborers to the Lord's money-making operations, and be loaded up with the next cargo of expensive and illicit goods to take away to the cities of the world. The corporations of this new world order were above the law, and in fact paid their stooges in the world's parliaments to make laws suitable for greater corporate profits. And the sheep of the world happily allowed themselves to be shackled up for the ride to their own oblivion.

Martin was still sobbing occasionally when the wheels underneath him touched down at a secret airstrip south of the Salton Sea. This was part of one of the world's largest desert systems—the Sonoran—that stretched from California across Arizona and much of New Mexico, and south across the border across a vast tract of northern Mexico. Nobody would ever think to look for them, and certainly nobody would report them as missing. The Lord's Church had chosen its penitent laborers very carefully. And a guy like Jimmy Sprocket might have himself enough drug money to stay wasted for the next month or two. The ways of the Lord were indeed mysterious.

Less than two hours after leaving the coast in the prison van, Martin and his fellow prisoners—still shackled, but now carrying their lightweight, sturdy chains—were allowed off the bus. The chauffeur rolled back the steel bars. The deacons assembled to keep their passengers in order.

Single-file, they climbed off the bus and onto a tarmac somewhere near the Mexican border.

Martin felt an icy wind ruffling his hair. This was high desert or something much like it.

Overhead, the Milky Way galaxy wheeled in frozen splendor, hundreds of millions of stars twinkling in a high, fast air current against an otherwise pitch-dark sky.

Deacon Ramirez announced in a deeply masculine, authoritative, and self-assured voice, "Welcome to the Lord Al-Balaam's Salton Sea Station, also known as the Triple-S-Ranch."

Deacon Beor added, "Thank you for your service."

Deacon Ramirez concluded, "Please file to my right into the main hangar, where you will receive work overalls. Your personal possessions will be placed in storage until the eventual release of your obligation, at which time be it years from now you will have the opportunity to reclaim your clothing for the ride back to the world."

By midnight, Martin found himself despairing ever more as he stood, wearing dark blue prison-like overalls, in a gigantic greenhouse. The air was filled with marijuana dust as well as exhaust fumes from tow motor vehicles moving huge bales around. Trucks came and went, loading cargo for transport to the cities of North America. Other trucks carried tons of marijuana (and probably hashish and opium poppies, Martin guessed) to the air strip for destinations around the world.

Martin was assigned to adjust bales of weed, which came rolled up like wall insulation or lawn insert turf strips. He and several other men and women wearing overalls, work gloves, and sturdy boots would make sure that each pallet had exactly sixteen bales on it, and that these were evenly distributed. When the tow motor came, or else a lifting crane depending on volume and scheduling, each pallet would be well-balanced and not spill its load as it was lifted onto a flatbed truck for transport.

Martin had managed to keep his wallet with him, smuggled from his street clothes into his socks during the clothing change in the hangar, and thence into the generous work pockets in the blue overalls. In the wallet were still his money, his I.D. cards, his driver's license, and his credit cards. That much he knew—he'd been able to quickly and surreptitiously check.

"Hey," said a low voice.

Martin looked up—startled—and saw a smallish, slender man of mixed race standing beside him.

"Don't look."

Martin didn't look, but listened.

"My name is Tony Cofoni. I am not here of my own free will. I take it you were Shanghaied."

"Yes. Is there hope of getting out of here?"

"Maybe. I've been here three months."

"Oh god." At the thought of missing Chloë, the interview, his entire future, Martin felt a dark storm of emotions raging all at once, from loss and grief to rage and violence. For the only time in his life, he experienced a sense of standing at the edge of an abyss. From here on, this was now or never, ever or forever, do or die.

"I need another man, and maybe you'll be it."

"What do we do?"

"Patience. Our shift gets off in thirty minutes. If we can pull this off, we may have a chance. They have armed guards all over the airport and the factory area. The fields and vineyards are out of the question. They also have security on all the roads and highways in the region."

"Wow," Martin said, "these cult leaders must have a lot of power."

"Money is more like it," said Tony. "Money is power. Wealth is everything. They are building more and more membership. They own people on the Highway Patrol, Migra, ICE, you name it. They own politicians in Washington; they own false news media. Control the medium, and you can make the message whatever you want it to be. Mix phony religion with dishonest politics, dismiss logic for emotion, and you have the world's many fools in your pocket." He added, "It's an endless propaganda cycle, a snowball effect—stir up fear, mix in anger, and you get hate. Add more fear, more anger, and you get more hate. Soon, you add violence to the hate. We are almost there in this society…"

"I'm in your hands," Martin said. *Oh god, let him not be another Jimmy Sprocket.*

"You can trust me," Tony said.

"I have no choice."

"Listen carefully. Act natural, like you are content to belong here. Stop crying and looking panicky. In about thirty minutes, make your way to the gate by the loading platform. I'll meet you there. It's fifty-fifty, but if we can get past the first step, we may have a chance of escaping."

"Otherwise?"

"We die trying. But anything is better than dying from old age in this prison of hell."

Chapter 8. Bombay Beach

At about midnight, it was shift change. A kind of foghorn blasted its message across the desert stillness, making a series of loud, throaty dinosaur mating calls that echoed for miles:

Ahhh!... (pause)... *Ahhh!...* (pause) *Ahhh!...* (pause)... *Ahhh!...* (pause) *Ahhh!...*

The siren went on like that for a full two minutes. It was the most frightening sound Martin could remember ever hearing. The blasts of sound were primeval, merciless, and terrifying.

Martin shuffled along with his group as a different set of people replaced them by the bales and piles and pallets.

The alleys among the piled and stacked product were lit by harsh bluish-white spotlights.

As one column of fresh workers arrived, Martin's column trudged tiredly toward what he presumed would be a barracks. He hoped not to find out. About twenty feet of him, amid other shadowy figures, walked the slender form of Tony Cofoni. All he had to do was follow the man, hopefully to freedom.

As they approached the main gate of the warehouse area, Tony swung to the right. Martin followed.

Martin glimpsed the world outside the warehouses, also controlled by the Church. He saw the industrial skyline of which Damual Shultz had spoken. But no time now for amazement or reverie. He hustled to follow Tony, who had a sprightly and determined step.

The path took Martin away from the bustle and into dark alleys among tall stacks of pallets. He was half afraid they would have dogs here, but it occurred to him that Al-Balaam would not want to slow the pace of operations to watch for a bunch of half-feral hunting hounds underfoot. That was why they had fences and armed guards. As the signs plainly indicated, the tall steel-mesh fences were electrified so a man could die of electrocution trying to scale their eighteen-foot height with barbed wire scrolled across the tops.

"Brown." It was Tony. "Over here."

Martin blinked several times and could not make out any detail in the darkness.

Tony took him by the wrist and pulled him into a niche among pallets. "We don't have much time, if any. I have some clothes here.

Dump those duds and let's become deacons."

Martin needed no persuasion. He was happy to shed his prison overalls for a size-too-large black suit, white shirt, and red bowtie. The pants were a bit too big, and he had to hold them by the belt with one hand.

Tony was already doffed out as Deacon Cofoni, Martin saw as his eyes became accustomed to the gloom.

Tony dusted Martin's shoulders. "You look great. Maybe we should join the Church and make some real money."

"No thanks."

"Just kidding."

"I hope so."

Side by side, they strode out from the darkness as if they belonged in their suits. "It's now or never, do or die," Tony said. He looked younger and more animated by the prospect of escaping from this vast criminal enterprise masquerading as a religious cult.

Martin worried that they might not be huge enough. The other deacons all seemed to be of football offensive lineman size.

Out of habit, he touched his wallet on his left buttock. It was still there, with its treasures.

"Make it look good," Tony muttered. "If we can get out the main gate, we have a chance."

They maintained a sure, steady pace to look as if they belonged in this game. Ordinary men and women in work overalls tended to make way and blend around them. As the wide gate approached, Martin's heart beat faster under his white shirt. If only...

"Bless the Lord," someone said.

"Amen," Martin said.

"So far so good," Tony muttered. "Steady now."

The gate was about seven yards across, Martin estimated. He saw three guard shacks—one on the left, one on the right, and one in the middle. Foot and motor traffic flowed thickly in on the left and out on the right. Just like street traffic in the world.

"This side is all that counts," Tony coached.

"Gentlemen," said a big Asian-American man in khaki uniform with black-billed hat, sporting an Uzi strapped across his chest.

"Bless us, Lord Al-Balaam," said Tony.

Two other guards similarly armed and attired stepped across their path.

"We are on the Lord's business," Martin said.

"Haven't seen you around," said the Asian guard.

Tony stopped and eyeballed him, a head lower. "I haven't seen you either. What's the password?"

The guard looked perplexed.

"I said, what's the password?"

Martin chimed in, "We say Oh Lord and you say—?"

"Al-Balaam?" the guard asked (stupidly, Martin thought).

"You got it. Good work," Tony said with a snap of the finger as he resumed walking, and Martin in step beside him.

"Keep up the good work, and Bless the Church," Martin said over his shoulder as they walked out into the freedom of a village owned and operated by the Church.

A glance back told Martin that the guards were not following them, but one was talking on a cell phone, and the other two stared inquisitively after them.

"We may only have a few minutes before they sound the alarm," Tony said.

"What now?"

"I had this all figured out, but it's already gone haywire. Don't stop, but listen. There is a village bus that comes by every fifteen minutes to pick Church people up and run them down to the village, where a lot of the lower-ranking staff live with their families. We can't stop and wait for the bus, and I don't know where it is. My timing must be off. So we have to just keep walking down into the village. Keep moving—that's our only hope."

"What will they do if they catch us?"

Tony shrugged. "Bread and water for a week, maybe, or they might kill us. Anything is possible. They are making billions of dollars on this drug business. They aren't going to let anything get between them and their money."

They paused for a moment to gain their bearings. They stood at the top of a low, broad hill. The main road in and out of the work compound led downhill to a mass of lights.

"That's the village," Tony said. "I've never been this far outside the compound, so I know little more than you do. It's small. I'm told there are maybe a thousand permanent residents."

"What is that shining band on the horizon?"

"That's the Salton Sea looking north. We're on a slight lagoon here that stretches into the desert. As near as I can make out, we are on the east side, which is sparsely populated. The Church has huge farms across the Mojave Desert, which we are ultimately in. The truck their product over here, package it—that's what you and I were doing—and ship it."

They resumed walking down the road toward the village. The lagoon between the village and the Salton Sea was camouflaged by stands of dry reeds, salt- and sun-bitten . The area smelled of dead fish and chemicals.

"I see that the village has a fence around it," Tony said. "Oh lord Balls or whatever. We may not make it out of here, but I sure don't want to go back."

"We could die trying to escape," Martin said. "Look, there is already an alarm out." He pointed downhill a quarter mile into the village, where red and blue lights flashed on top of a police car. "I wonder if they are looking for us."

"I don't want to find out," Tony said.

"How did you get sucked into this?" Martin asked.

"They hired me as a gardener, those people where you were kidnapped. I had no idea what a bunch of nuts and crooks these people are until one day, I happened to see a man and a woman going at it in the gardens. They have about three acres behind the church, mostly walkways and little flower beds and bushes. There they were, naked as jaybirds, humping away and making noise. Well, it turns out the guy was Reverend Damual Shultz, and the chick was the daughter of a wealthy patron. These guys are funded by billionaires all the way out to Shanghai, Bombay, Sao Paolo, you name it. So they couldn't let me rat on the holy reverend phony, and here I am. They claim I stole a thousand dollars from a Church kitty."

"And that's a lie of course?" Martin asked. Something about the odd, fractured light in Tony's eyes told him the truth lay somewhere inbetween. Clearly—when it came to money—such people became ruthless sociopaths.

"Of course," Tony said with a sideways glance, a little tic or twitch that belied his denial.

Having been burned by his trust in Marsha Starker and Jimmy Sprocket, Martin resolved to work with Tony—he had no choice—and yet to verify while following.

"Duck!" Tony said and pulled Martin into the shadows amid a grove of trees.

A second later, a private security car came flying past with flashing lights and keening siren.

"They are after us," Martin guessed.

"We have to assume so," Tony said.

"What can we do?" He felt ice cold waves like gravel in his gut. He was prepared to do just about anything to escape. Freedom beckoned on the horizon in all directions except back—so near, yet so far.

Tony tugged at his sleeve. "Look." He pointed through the copse of trees and yuccas in which they stood. Off to the side, away from the road, were more lights. "That is a compound," Tony said. "If my hunch is right, that is the upscale side of town. That's where Reverend Shultz comes to entertain and play."

"I do hear laughter," Martin said.

"I hear shattering glass, like beer bottles being thrown. And splashing, like people in and out of that Olympic-size pool behind the mansion over there. Let's scout around."

The path away from the main road, through the yucca stand, took them out on a rolling green golf course. Signs posted read *Church Property* and *No Trespassing.*

"We've come to the right place," Tony said. "Nobody would expect we'd run into the fire rather than out of the barn."

Martin nodded, looking back the way they'd come. He saw several security cars with flashing lights on the other side of the road. "They're already beating the bushes over there, on the assumption we'd take the quickest path."

"That leads to barbed wire and electrified fencing. We'd be dead already."

Together, Martin and Tony strode across the dark grass. Martin hoped to avoid twisting an ankle in a gopher hole or any sort of golfing trap, whatever those were called.

As they drew near the two-story, sprawling estate, they saw an amazing sight. Behind the estate lay a huge swimming pool that glowed bluish-aqua in the night. About forty or fifty people milled about, having a cookout. One could smell beer and wine, and the occasional whiff of weed, all the way up on the golf course.

Strangest of all, the Deacons (Ramirez and Beor) reclined in beach chairs, wearing only swimming trunks. Their hands were folded on their bellies, they grinned from ear to ear, and each was being vigorously fellated by his own attractive cheerleader-type woman in a bikini.

"Family values," Martin said.

"Don't do what I do, do what I say," Tony said. "Hypocrites."

Martin shook his head, thinking of the people slaving in the compound or out on the marijuana plantations and vineyards. "And all these fools up there are doing years of penance to save the world from sin by throwing their lives away."

"Figures. That's the best way to control the masses, and this is a laboratory experiment. Misguided faith and dishonest politics, and you got Reverend Shultz high on weed, getting a blow job."

"We've got to get out of this place."

"You're telling me. This is your first day. I've been in this living hell for three months."

As they drew closer, they saw that the Church leaders' compound was surrounded by a tall, electrified fence. "No way in," Martin said. "Not that we'd want to go in."

"Makes it harder for them to get out and find us," Tony said. "I'm praying they are all high on weed like those two deacons.

Just then, Martin heard a loud scream. He was startled.

But it was just the Reverend Shultz, stark-naked with this wang flapping in the breeze, running to escape three naked women who were screaming with laughter and waving champagne bottles. The four of them plunged into the deep end in an explosion of screaming, laughter, and chlorinated foam.

"Looks like fun," Tony said bitterly.

"Our time is running out," Martin said.

"Look, there is a small marina." Tony pointed down to the reed-choked waterfront. The fenced-in estate extended to within about two hundred feet of a muddy, slimy looking beach that looked like a swamp if anything.

"The Salton Sea is polluted, dirty, and dying," Martin said.

"I read that too. Let's see if we can heist a boat."

They walked along a wooden plank pier that stretched out over the marsh. Frogs burruped all around, and the air was shrill with constant cricket noise.

"There's a light on in the shack," Tony said.

Sure enough, at the end of the pier, where about four boats of various types and sizes were tied up, was a guard shack or boat house. Not only was a light on, but two men in khaki uniforms stood together talking, smoking cigarettes, and looking toward the joy and noise up at the mansion.

"We can't go forward, and we can't go backward," Martin said.

"Can you swim?"

"Moderately."

"Good enough. That's very salty water. We'll be buoyant. Let's try to sneak past the guards, slip into the water, and gently scissor-kick out of hearing range. Then we can get on our bellies and swim like hell."

Martin shook his head. "I'm afraid we have no choice."

Seeing an empty plastic bag that had once held sliced bread, he packaged his wallet and cell phone to keep them dry. Whatever else happened, he would keep this bag close at hand.

"If we're lucky, a passing boat will pick us up once we are out of the lagoon. Hopefully not from the Church."

"Let's not waste any time," Martin said. "I hope there are no sharks or crocodiles in that water."

"Just human ones," Tony said.

They stripped down to their shorts and T-shirts, hiding the deacon suits in muck and reeds.

Keeping behind the shack, where there were no windows for the guards to spot them, they waded out into the water. Martin had his work boots on. He was grateful not to feel the slime and muck between his toes. The boots sucked in water and slowed him down a bit.

"When we get out there," Tony suggested, "let's kick off the boots and swim for it."

"Deal."

Behind them, the tone of the festivities changed somewhat.

"Our absence has been noticed," Martin said. He heard a radio playing loudly. The news was on, and a woman announcer's voice drifted across the lagoon. Her words were amplified and clarified by the water. "Police in the San Diego area are on the lookout for a possible psychopath named Angry or Angus or even Henry Bitters, middle name something like Story or Sturdy, who allegedly hacked a woman to death on a county beach during the evening's ferocious storm. Details are scarce, but residents of San Diego, Riverside, and Orange Counties are urged to remain on alert and exercise extreme caution. Every police agency is actively searching. Marine Corps squads are combing beaches up and down San Diego County, looking for evidence. The suspect is described as...." The announcer went on to offer a reasonable descriptive facsimile of Martin.

This was not lost on Tony. His eyes widened, and his face

looked alarmed.

"I'm not the killer," Martin blurted, but regretted saying anything.

"Eeek!" Tony shrieked, back-paddling away from Martin.

"Did you steal the money?"

"What?"

"I've been wondering."

"No—that's a lie they made up."

"Good. Well, I didn't kill anyone, ever, in my entire life."

"Stay away from me."

"We can't afford to screw each other over, Tony."

"Okay," he bargained. "We escape this hellhole together. After that, we split up."

"Fair enough. You're too ugly for me to look at anyway."

Silently, they launched forth and began dog paddling as the water deepened. There was a quarter moon in a clear sky, so they had just enough light to make out minimal details around them. That water glittered and the swamp didn't.

"My god," Tony said. "Look."

To their right was a boat, moored to a short wooden pier by a heavy rope.

Martin swam closer for a look. "What kind of boat is this? Like a toy."

Tony emerged from the water, pulling himself up on the gunwale with a soft hiss of water. "It's a speed boat with one seat in the middle. How odd."

"Not too odd," Martin said. "Look. That pier is a ski ramp. This is the Reverend Modesty's little water-skiing toy. I'm surprised he doesn't have a wet bar up here on the pier."

"One of us could ride out on it and get help."

"Not on your life," Martin said. "We're in this together to the bitter end. Besides, we are still so close the motor sound would give us away. I have an idea though."

"I'm up for anything," Tony said. "Almost anything." Martin noticed that Tony kept his distance now that they'd heard the radio news story about a supposed psycho killer on the loose.

They loosened the boat. Martin pulled the water skis down and propped them across the stern. The long tow rope was coiled in a well in the stern.

Together, they held onto the boat—which made for a good

support, in any case—and paddled with their feet in tandem. That gained them good distance in a short while.

"Have you ever water skied?" Martin asked.

"Are you serious? I'm from the big city back east. I can barely stand up in the shallow end of a pool, much less swim."

"Okay, then you drive, and I'll ski." Martin was a modestly able swimmer, and he had never surfed, but he'd tried water skiing a few times long ago, and had a reasonable feel for the sport.

A while later, they were past the reeds and in the open sea, which was really more of a smelly lake covered with slime.

With some effort, Tony climbed into the boat and got the motor started, while Martin uncoiled the rope and hung back. He held the tow rope with both hands, and kept his boards pointed upward ready to go.

And go they did. With an explosive engine roar, Tony got the boat moving. "We have to get out of here!" he yelled. "Hang on!"

And so, with Tony piloting the boat, Martin ended up slaloming behind on the boat's wake. It was shaky going if you were not in practice and barely knew what you were doing. A few times, yelling "Who-aah!" Martin almost pitched forward or backward. He almost lost control a few times.

For about fifteen minutes, they churned steadily northward. It was extra hard to keep a footing in the dark, not to mention the churning waves and a certain amount of zigzagging. Was Tony trying to lose him?

Sure enough, as the lights of a settlement (perhaps Bombay Beach?) hove into sight on their right—the eastern shore—Tony turned around and began loosening the tow line. He steered with his left had while undoing the line, and there was nothing Martin could do. If nothing else, they had escaped from the Church of Al-Balaam. Now he could make his way north or northwest to Los Angeles, and recover his sanity.

Tony Cofoni favored him with one long, looping pass along the shore. Martin came loose and sank into the waves, while Tony roared off into the night, never to be seen again.

At this point, Martin was just glad to be alive and free.

Wearing only briefs and a T-shirt, he swam ashore. He wanted to throw himself flat on his face, but the sand here reeked of dying mussels and was foamy with some chemical that smelled like the plant that had disgorged it from its discharge pipes. Holding his plastic bag with wallet and cell phone, he waded on shore and kept walking. He was barefoot, and the profusion of broken, sweet-water shells cut into his soles, but he must make it to the road. He did find one discarded, torn plastic flip-flop sandal, which he shifted alternately between his left and right feet. At times he hopped on the sandal foot; at other time, on the bare foot. Eventually, he made it to the narrow macadam road. Under a single light in the middle of nowhere, he examined the contents of his plastic bag.

The cell phone appeared to be working. It was receiving signal. Sending, like calling Chloë, might be a different matter. It was now almost two in the morning.

Then he checked the contents of his wallet, and felt his stomach sink.

The money, credit cards, driver's license, and other items were all gone. The wallet had been padded with bits of plain cardboard to fool him. Either Jimmy Sprocket had already robbed him at the Church, while selling him into slavery, or the elders might have taken his stuff. Or even Tony, who had an opportunity in the shadows when they were changing into deacon costumes. It didn't matter who or how—the deed was done, and he was now officially not only homeless, but on the run from every law enforcement agency in Southern California.

Second worst case, he might be shot dead on sight like a coyote on a chicken farm.

Worst of all, Chloë might never see him again if she believed any of this.

Chapter 9. Air Mail

Barefoot, nearly naked, limping, Martin staggered along a dark road lit only by a quarter moon. In one hand, he clutched his cell phone. It was his only lifeline to the normal world.

To his left lay the smelly expanse of the Salton Sea. Martin had studied its meaning in school. The Salton Sea was a man-made body of water, the world's largest lake fifteen miles across east-to-west, thirty-five miles north-to-south—but accidentally created by human error. In 1905, a dam on the Colorado River had broken, flooding the dry Salton lake bed with gadzillions of gallons of water over two years. The dam had been repaired, but the entire region continued draining into this now stagnant pool of water for over a century. It lay just five feet above the ground level of Death Valley to its north, both of them on the San Andreas Fault. The Salton Sea drained all the industrial and farming poisons created by corporations and sheltered by crooked politicians.

Martin stood at the edge of this alien sea, and with a mighty wail of despair, threw his wallet with its cardboard contents far into the turgid algae blooms.

This was no longer earth but an alien world inverse-engineered to become a poisonous exoplanet. It had become an alternate earth populated by freaks and producers, by knife-wielding psycho ladies and bicycling sprocket monsters.

Could one ever trust another soul? Worse than having your wallet, your possessions, and your very identity stolen was not knowing who had done it.

Was Jimmy Sprocket passing himself off as Martin Brown after bicycling to Los Angeles and ominously rapping his knuckles on an unsuspecting Chloë's door at three a.m.?

Was Tony Cofoni pretending to be Martin Brown while entering secret rocket installations in Pomona to sabotage earth's last chance of reaching outer space before the Big Bloom spread from Salton Sea across all the world's oceans, creating a race of ravenous, staggering zombie blob people with extended arms and limply dangling fingers?

As he stood by the sea, he punched in Chloë's phone number. He had been afraid, knowing neither she nor anyone else would believe him about any of these events. Now he must speak with her.

First, he listened to his recorded, downloaded messages. There was a short text from Chloë,

> Martinwhere R U?
> Waiting so anxious.
> Love / Chloë

Then he tried to answer.
All he got was an unhappy-face symbol meaning,

> Out of range.

He would have to hold that thought and try again later as he got within range of decent cell service.

Am I hallucinating?

As Martin staggered along that black-asphalt, macadam road in the night, with a citric yellow quarter moon hanging in the sky above like a hilarious laugh-mouth amid starry sprinkles of delirious happiness, he thought he heard voices.

Out here, in the middle of nowhere, at the edge of the world?

He heard a clattering sound that almost sounded like the big brewery horses in the annual Rose Bowl Parade, except it was pitch dark, there wasn't a brewery for miles, and this was the beginning of an alien, alternate earth.

Yo buddy, whatcha been smokin'?

As he heard those words, Martin dreamed that he was surrounded by cowboys, and he pitched forward unconscious onto his face. Brutal asphalt, still warm from the day's heat and smelling like oil and vegetable soup. smashed his nose like a giant fist.

"Take it easy," said a deep male voice with a Texas drawl. "Yore gonna be fahne, podnah."

Martin blinked his eyes open—first one, then the other.

He swayed back and forth as if he were on a tiny boat in a gale at sea. Only he was strapped by the legs onto a saddle, and the swaying came from a huge horse's ass right underneath him. His arms were wrapped around a woman's waist. His hands apparently had been tied together before her belly, because he was firmly strapped in place.

"Don't worry," said the woman. Her flannel shirt felt warm, her skin soft, and Martin gratefully rested his cheek against her firm but yielding flesh. "We found you wandering by the road. We're doing to take you home and feed you and take care of you."

Oh god, what if they are cannibals? Anything is possible tonight. What if they eat me?

On another horse nearby rode a cowboy man with a wide hat and a weather-beaten face. "Take it easy, *podnah*. Yore troubles are over. Whar ya from, *podnah*?"

"I want to go to Los Angeles," Martin said with a mouth full of cotton, or so it felt.

"What did he say?" the cowboy asked.

The woman replied, "He says he warned us about those amperes."

"That doesn't make sense."

"It's electrical talk, Robby. You wouldn't understand."

"And you do?"

"I am an alchemist. Whatever he says is very arcane and powerful."

"You think he's a shaman?"

"Or a lost soul. We'll find out soon when Gramma talks to him. He needs shoes, lunch, and love."

"Somebody please help me," Martin said. He was slumped forward, staring at the passing road surface, which looked like a continuous streak of gravel in soft moonlight. A blur of clattering horse hooves framed that vision on all sides.

"What did he say?" the cowboy asked. He hadd an ancient repeating rifle slung over one shoulder.

"He says his body was in the kelp, and he had to pee. That must be why he came ashore."

"You think he's one of the monsters that live in that polluted swamp out there?"

"He seems pretty human to me," the woman said.

As she spoke, Martin heard a howling, laughing sound that echoed eerily under the starry sky. Another voice answered somewhere on the horizon, heard through the raised arms of cacti and Joshua trees. Martin's skin crawled. What was that?

"Coyotes," said the cowboy, raising his rifle with a clatter of metal parts. "Probably some wolves out there too. The federal gummint's been releasing wolves out here to hunt us down."

"Oh shush," said the woman. "You been listening to that False News too much. They'll tell you any old corporate lies to get you paranoid out of your skin so you hate the gummint."

The cowboy said, "Listen to you. Imaginary corporations. What next? UFOs. Aliens."

"Alchemy," she said. "Pure and simple. Secret lore of the ages."

Martin woke up, bit by bit, and realized he was being rescued by a pack of riders of the purple sage. There were a half dozen. He counted four men and two women. The other woman was slender and dark-haired, dressed like a Native American in buckskin tunic and sandals. Her hair was braided on the sides, and held by colorful bead ties.

"Here we are," said the cowboy, as they rode into a trailer camp.

"You okay back there?" the woman said kindly. "My name is Xena. That's like Seenah with an X."

"How do you do?" Martin said. "Can someone untie me?"

The cowboy sidled close on his horse. Brandishing a very large and dangerous looking bush-knife with a serrated back and a glinting blade, he said, "Don't try nuttin' funny or I'll gut you like one o' them kaiyotes." With one powerful tug of a gnarled hand, he pulled on the knots and Martin's ropes fell loose.

Martin nearly fell out of the saddle, but helpful hands caught him.

The People, as they called themselves, helped him down. His legs were a bit shaky, but he managed to stagger with their help. They led him toward the middle trailer of several parked amid sage brush and tumbleweeds against a landscape of cactus, rolling purple mountains, and starry galaxies.

"Stick with me," Xena said as she helped him along. The others took their horses, including Xena's, and with suspicious after-glances, led the animals away to water and feed.

The Indian woman and Xena held Martin's elbows and helped him up the stairs into a double-wide mobile home that smelled severely of cats. Someone had once told Martin that places inhabited by old men smell of old men, whereas places inhabited by old women smell of cats. It was a law of nature.

"Who is this?" asked an elderly woman wearing a bluish *muumuu*. She fluffed her dress out with both hands while twisting her ample torso in slight corkscrewing motions.

"We found him wandering on the shore road," Xena said.

"He's either lost or nuts, or both," said the Native American woman. It was the first time Martin heard her speak.

"Sit him down here," said the older woman.

"But Gramma, that's your chair."

"'Ay nayds it more than I dew," said the woman. She spoke with a Cockney accent, swallowing her syllables wholesale.

Martin was feeling better already. "Thank you."

"He spoke," said the Native American woman. "My name is Ana Diegueno."

"How do you do?" Martin said. "Are we safe?"

Ana and Xena both laughed. "Of course. What ever do you mean by that?"

Martin saw his reflection in an open closet door mirror in the crowded but homey little trailer. He had wide, horrified eyes, a gaping mouth that seemed frozen in a scream, and a bloody nose from falling face-first on the road.

"This is Gramma," said Xena as the older woman came rushing with a warm washcloth.

Gramma clucked and fussed as she gently wiped crusted dirt and blood from Martin's nose. "Does it 'urt, boybee?"

Martin nodded. "I don't know if I broke it."

"'Ow did ja do that?" Gramma asked while dabbing.

"He fell flat on his face," said Xena, "just when we reached him." She brought him a set of men's black sweats—pants and a shirt. He modestly climbed into them. They fit well enough.

Ana handed him a pair of cowboy boots, belonging to one of the men, and those fit him well.

"I escaped from bad people," Martin said, glad to no longer be near naked. He resumed his seat.

"He's hallucinating for sure," Ana said. She covered him with a blanket. "Get warm, dear."

"What bad people, hon?" Gramma asked. She slipped into a more comfortable U.S. dialect.

"Church. Growing weed."

Xena burst out laughing. "There are all sorts of crazy people living around here. You must have had a run-in with some flying saucer loonies."

"We are the sane ones," Ana said.

"Don't be scared," Gramma said. "I came here half a century ago with the hippies. I was one of the original Mersey Sound girls who came over with the Beatles. I joined a commune and found peace here at the Salton Sea when it turned stinky and all the tourists left. Nothing bad has ever happened here. It's the land of love."

"Thank you," Martin said sincerely. He relaxed a bit. He put his cowboy boots up and crossed his legs at the ankles, careful not to get the foot rest dirty. He prayered his hands over his belly. "I'm trying to reach my girlfriend in LA."

"You have a girlfriend in LA," Gramma said. "How sweet." She held the rag aside, examined her handiwork, and nodded. "I don't think it's broken. Just bruised."

Xena said, "I'll put a plastic strip over it."

"And some antibiotic ointment," Ana said.

"Not really a girlfriend yet," Martin said. "More of a girl friend at this point." Seeing the disappointed looks on the women's faces, he added, "I think we are on the verge of love—a life-long love like in a romance novel." He added, "The clean kind, without sex scenes." He added, "Yet."

"That is so sweet," Ana said. "Is she a Native American girl by any chance?"

"I'm not sure. Her name is Chloë and she works near UCLA."

"UCLA! A brain, huh? You look sort of like a professor or a movie producer."

"Not a producer," Martin said, feeling a hint of panic.

"We'll getcha fixed right up," Gramma said. "You need a ride to LA?"

Martin nodded. Was it possible? "The cowboys?"

Gramma shook her head. "The boys are too superstitious to come in here. We women do our magic in here. The boys stay out with the horses."

"I love magic," Martin said.

"You can stay in here as long as you want," said Ana as she

brought a tray full of medicines and herbs. "We can pray over you."

"Whatever you wish," Martin said, while thinking, *Just no slave marijuana plantations oh god I beg you please and I am not addressing my prayer to Al-Balaam.*

Gramma said, "My great-granddaughter is a member of the local Girl Guides troop. You call them Girl Scouts. It just happens they are leaving for an all-day powwow up in Death Valley. I'm sure they can squeeze you in at least as far as Mecca or even Suicide Rock."

Martin felt a new throb of panic. "What?"

Xena laughed as she cleaned Martin's nose with a fresh, damp, warm terry cloth and Ana waited to apply ointment with a hovering fingertip. "It's all a bunch of legend."

Gramma clucked as she puttered about the sink in the small, cluttered mobile home. "This country is filled with legends of a Native princess who fell in love with the wrong man. They were hated by society, and jumped to their deaths off Suicide Rock holding hands."

Martin could picture them in his writer's vision: *…The girl's dress fluttering against a beautiful inky blue night sky, her pigtails curled upward, the young man's muscular arms spread, and maybe an eagle soaring over a full moon that looks like a huge golden coin amid dark clouds nearby. Oh god I have to get to LA and write this story. Chloë will love its. We will cry together.*

"Every state has its own variation," Gramma said. "We have them in England too, dating to Anglo-Saxon and Druid times before the invaders came."

"The invaders," Martin said. It was a question.

"The Romans," Gramma explained. "The corporations. They have taken over the world, bit by bit. First they were the Romans, then the Church, and later the Reformation to finish it all off. They invented the Industrial Revolution to replacing Neolithic farming cultures."

Xena explained, "My Granddad, the hippie, was a history professor. He died long ago, but Gramma still tells some of his stories."

Ana added, "Most of it's way over our heads."

Martin nodded. "Do you have any water?" He licked his lips.

"Poor thing," Gramma said. "I'll make you some tea. You must be parched."

"Put a little ginseng in it for him," Ana said.

"Would you like that?" Gramma asked as if Martin were a child.

He nodded fervently. "Caffeinated, if possible. Yes, please. I have to make it through the night."

Gramma patted him on the chest with a heavy hand, while rising to do as he asked. "A witches' brew, coming right up for ya!"

Martin closed his eyes and relaxed for a few minutes as best he could. The women fussed around the kitchen.

"Put on the telly if you wish," Gramma said. She handed him an antique-looking control wand, pushing the On button with a grimy thumb.

Martin held the control against his chest while the television swam into life.

The news was on, showing pictures of a beach in San Diego. "Police are looking for..."

Martin jerked the Off button, instantly making the TV go blank.

"What happened?" Ana asked.

"The news makes me cry," Martin said. His neck prickled with sudden sweat. He must not be mistaken for the Beach Killer.

Gramma enthused, "You really are a hippie. So sensitive. You should think about bringing Zoë here to live with us."

Chloë, Martin thought. *I can imagine us jumping off Suicide Rock together. No thanks.*

Xena smiled while wiping freshly washed dishes with a towel. "If you were gay, it could be Joey."

Martin shook his head—anxiously.

"He's all nervous," Ana said. "Don't tease him so."

The door opened, and up the steps climbed a gorgeous young women in her teens.

"Oh, Carmela," Ana said. "Have you heard about Martin?"

Carmela fastened hungry, inquisitive teenage eyes on Martin. She seemed to devour him with her thoughts. Was he nice? Was he safe? Did he like her? *Darker thoughts...*

Carmela stood in the doorway, transfixed and staring at Martin. She had long dark glossy hair, pale skin, and large, luminous eyes that were brown verging on a lovely inky-blue night sky glow. She was slender, and wearing a sort of grayish, English-style Girl Guides uniform. That included hiking boots, gray crew socks, army blanket green (olive drab) shorts, an off-color grayish blue shirt open and rumpled at the collar, and a striped neck-kerchief in alternating

California state colors of azure and gold.

Martin was impressed. This young woman had a certain *je ne sais quois* beauty, aura, atmosphere, whatever, like Chloë in a way though younger and out of bounds.

Behind Carmela pressed several other young women dressed in GIGs outfits. Some were blonde, others dark-haired, but Martin immediately cottoned to their refreshingly honest faces, good will, and total mix of all races and persuasions.

"Come on in, girls," said Gramma. "We invented the Girl Guides over in England, you know. Old Baden-Powell back in the day. You call them Girl Scouts just to be different. Old Baden-Powell in 1909 wanted a separate movement for girls, so they invented guiding for girls only. I thought we needed something like that here in the Bombay Beach area, but they call themselves Girl Scouts in the US manner, and there we are. Are you ready to go, girls?"

Carmela said in a sweet, thin voice, "Yes, Gramma. You want us to take this gentleman with us?"

"He was heading toward LA."

Carmela smiled mysteriously. "We can help him on his way then."

Xena said, "Are you ready to go, Martin? We don't want to keep the Girl Scouts waiting, do we?"

Oh god get me out of here and on my way, Martin thought as he pushed himself out of the chair.

Ana thumped him on the back. "So long, Martin. Bring Chloë back to see us sometime."

"Thank you for everything," Martin said to Xena, Ana, and Gramma.

The women wished him off in a chorus of cheers and pleasantry.

"This way," Carmela said. She pointed with a delicate hand. Everything about her was petite—her cute, shapely legs; her sweet little arms; her delicate neck and girlish features. And those large, ambient eyes...

A van stood by the trailer park. It did not bear any sort of scary Church markings, but rather a very commonplace car rental logo.

"We can fit you in," a slightly heavier, more honey-skinned girl said. She had long black hair parted in the middle and combed out so it fell in thick, glossy bluish-black locks over her shoulders.

All the girls wore uniforms similar to Carmela's, though none was exactly the same as the other. It made for a nice spark of individuality.

"Thank you so much," Martin said. "I am so grateful."

"Been through an ordeal?" asked the Hispanic girl.

"Looks like you were in a brawl," said a cute little Filipina in calf-length corduroy deck pants. She touched Martin's face with delicate fingertips.

They walked him to the van, about a dozen young women, all relaxed and chattering pleasantly.

"Go on," Carmela said, and Martin followed her pointing finger up into the bus. Remembering his last experience, he sat as close to the door as he could—behind the driver's seat.

The van was already loaded with backpacks and duffel bags. A few cheerful pennants were visible, along with a cardboard sign that said Jamboree. The letters on the sign were decorated with little flowers and a cute butterfly.

"I will be driving," Carmela told Martin, "since I am eighteen and the oldest."

"I am sure you are a very safe driver," Martin said.

"Thank you for your confidence in me." She waved both arms in circular motions over her knees, signaling for the girls to hurry up and board.

People at the trailer park, including several cowboys and a few aging hippies with graying hair and headbands, cheered and waved goodbye.

"See you in a few days!" Carmela said, waving from the driver's side window.

Presently, the van pulled out onto the road, and sailed along the Salton Sea with music playing loudly—a nice mix of pop tunes, a little rap, some hip-hop and Mex, plus salsa and a little manilla-vanilla. The girls chatted light-heartedly about school, boyfriends, rock stars, pets, pink things, and—what else?—shopping.

Carmela and the Mexican girl Lorena had a more grown-up conversation with Martin.

"Where are you going again?" he asked.

"Big Jamboree in Death Valley," Lorena said. "That's a Scouting convention. We all camp out, sing songs, and play games."

"Tell stories," Carmela continued the thought, "talk about scouting history, learn camping and first aid skills."

"Sounds like a lot of fun," Martin said. "How do I get from there to Los Angeles?"

"We can drop you off at a bus station," Carmela said.

"Here," Lorena said, fingering a cell phone. "Let me check. I'll look at a map."

Martin waited, noticing that several of the girls would chatter together, sometimes hiding their words behind a sheltering hand, and glance toward him with conspiratorial eyes. It was almost as if they were plotting something.

"This is very straightforward," Lorena said. "We are heading north on California State Road 84."

Martin looked outside, seeing dark desert flying past under a quarter moon.

"Past Coachella, near Indio, we'll pick up U.S. Interstate 10. That hooks north around Loma Linda and San Bernardino, on the 215, which connects with Interstate 15 going north toward Nevada."

Carmela said, while holding the wheel and driving, "That's right. So what's the best road for him?"

Lorena consulted her map again. "If he stays on Interstate 10, that will take him directly into Los Angeles, about two hours away from San Bernardino."

"Perfect," Carmela said. To Martin she added, "All your troubles are over."

"Do you have money for the bus?" Lorena asked.

Martin grimaced. He was embarrassed to admit he was broke, but what choice did he have? "Actually, I was robbed and I have nothing anymore, not even my wallet or my driver's license."

"That is so awful," Carmela said.

"You poor guy," Lorena added with a sad look. She turned to the girls in back and said loudly, "Ladies, Mr. Brown was robbed. He has no money, and his wallet is gone. What can we do?"

The girls all stared at Martin.

The bus grew silent, and Martin got a shiver up and down his spine at the intensity of their gaze. One girl seemed to be drooling, and wiped delicate, cute little fingers across her quivering lips.

"We're thinking," Carmela said disarmingly, while concentrating on the driving. The wheel looked huge in her small arms, but she bounced in the driver's seat with confidence, poise, and joy.

"We might take up a collection," Lorena said.

"Yes, a collection," said Carmela.

One or two of the Girl Guides moved up closer, with a certain dark eagerness that struck Martin as being just a bit too intense for a feeling of wanting to help a stray homeless man.

"Your girlfriend is in movies?" one girl asked.

Martin nodded. "She is actually my—oh well, yes, I'm in love with her."

They all rolled their eyes up and made a chorus of dreamy voices. "Ohhhhh...how beautiful."

As the van rolled on, they began to look ever more other-worldly. They looked ever more similar in some mysterious, stirring way that Martin could not quite grasp. Especially their eyes seemed so large, with white sclera and dark pupils, a lot like the moon swimming amid clouds at night.

"Can we stop for refreshment?" asked one girl.

"Yes," said another, "I'm really thirsty."

"Gotta go potty," said a third.

"Okay, ladies," Lorena announced. "We'll take a rest stop. Gramma packed us a little extra refreshment for the long road ahead."

"I see a road stop ahead," Carmela said.

"Something nice and private," Lorena suggested.

"Oh goody," said the drooling girl.

Another girl held both hands to her mouth and seemed to be licking her palms in eager anticipation.

"I gotta pee, myself," Martin said quietly to Carmela.

Time to run.

"I'm sure you will find a nice, dark, secluded little spot in the woods," Lorena said with an undisguised eagerness. She seemed to also be drooling, and quickly cupped a hand over her red lips.

Time to hie up your ass and start jogging, brother.

Martin had been taken for enough rides in one evening. He sensed this might be another one.

"Here we go," Carmela said as she eased the van off the road, onto a sandy, gravely shoulder in a deserted stretch.

As the van slowly rolled to a stop, the girls seemed increasingly eager—out of control.

"I want a sip," said one.

"Bite me," said another.

One girl slapped another. "Keep your thangs to yourself, bitch!"

Martin wondered if he'd misheard. Had she said *things* or *fangs?*

Carmella pulled the van into a parking lot lit at either end by an overhead bare bulb, each under a tin shade. It was a small rest area with a brick building in the middle marked Men and Women at opposite ends.

When the engine was off, they all heard a rattling sound. It was a grinding sound, like knives being loudly sharpened, up and down, blood-curdling, with screaming voices in the background if you heard it just so and so. Martin grew even more alarmed.

"What's that?" asked a girl.

Carmela said, "Sounds like a train. There is a rail line near here. Runs into Coachella and Palm Desert, I think. Sounds like they are slowing down because they'll be in the station soon."

Lorena reached over and ran a hand over Carmela's bare arm. The tip of Lorena's tongue protruded over blood-red lips that looked so full and beautiful that Martin was almost hypnotized, as if there were an aphrodisiac floating in the air.

Carmela pulled into the rest stop in the middle, away from the lights.

"I've really gotta go badly," Martin said.

"He'll pee in the van," said a girl in the back.

Martin heard their voices but the girls were an indistinct mob of blobs in the gloom.

"Let him go."

"He'll be back in a minute," said a third voice.

"We can wait."

Carmela said, "Oh look, there is a woman getting out of that SUV."

There was a stir as several girls moved in a frantic, eager pack to put their fingertips on the window and stare outside. Martin saw Lorena licking her lips. Had her lips begun to transform? Were her eyes growing blacker and more liquid? And Carmela—she stared with luminous, ravenous eyes at a businesswoman who had stepped from her SUV and was about to use the womens' side of the brick structure. She was a plain, slightly heavy woman of about forty with thick glasses and a beret, wearing a dark red skirt and white high heels.

"That red color just turns me on," said one of the girls in back in a husky, drooly tone.

Martin felt something warm on his arm and looked down, just in time to see an eager young face staring up at him with wide open night eyes gleaming with liquid thirst. The girl had just licked his arm with a warm, wet tongue like a cat's, seeking the scent of blood, relishing the foretaste of a good wine.

Martin bobbed to his feet like a cork. "I have to go to the Men's room."

"Go ahead," Carmela said. She flicked a switch and the door sighed open. "We'll be here waiting for you."

Martin stepped from the van, desiring to never set foot in it again.

Night wind sighed around his neck and hair, bringing with it a winey scent of warm night pines that had basked in sunlight all day. The desert had its unique smells that no city dweller could fathom.

Faking it, Martin walked briskly toward the door market Men. The sign glowed wanly under the nearby lamp under its shade.

Gravel crunched under his feet.

Did he dare duck around the corner and start running? Would they be after him like a swarm of starving, thirsty bats? How fast were teenage vampire girls anyway, when they had to chase down some helpless prey that was running for its life?

Chickening out, Martin ducked into the men's room to think. He had to pee really badly, and unzipped over a stainless steel urinal. The structure was brick outside, concrete inside, built for simplicity, durability, and cleanliness. The smell wasn't too bad.

Sure, he thought while peeing with shaky hands and waving spout, *that's because hardly anyone ever comes here.*

He had only seconds, he figured, before one of them would not be able to contain her thirst any longer and come looking for him.

He spotted an open window. There—his only hope. He stood on a wooden bench, pushed the mosquito screen away, and threw himself out head-first.

He landed, with a somersault, on his feet. For a moment, he thought he had broken his neck. But it was just a jarring fall. His feet landed on thick pine needles. He was out!

On the rear side of the brick shithouse was only dark pine forest. He heard the grinding noises of the train, somewhere on the other side of these dense pine trees.

Martin darted forward, cautiously at first.

Before disappearing into the black pine forest, he caught a glimpse of the parking lot. There was the van, looking ominous and scary in its parking space. All the girls were still inside, but for how long?

He saw the woman in the red dress, slumped on the rim of a bench that surrounded a huge flower pot in which sat a small tree. Carmela was holding the woman in a lover's embrace. The woman's pale arms lay limply by her sides, draping down from a slumped torso. The woman looked as if she were asleep, with a peaceful smile on her face. At her neck was Carmela, delicate but wiry, strong and deadly, as she sang long ivory teeth-fangs into the woman's soft and vulnerable flesh, looking for a fat, juicy red jugular vein.

Behind her stood Lorena, who cradled her arms around herself and trembled with anticipation, awaiting her turn at seconds or leftovers. Lorena's full, dark red lips had become engorged, and white fangs protruded over them while her large, liquid eyes swam with the blackness of eternal night.

Oh fuck what next?

Martin ran for his life.

Behind him he heard an outcry—a chorus of young girl voices raised in the wind—and he knew they had figured out he was splitting. He was making like a tree and leaving. He was faking a banana and splitting.

The quarter moon provided almost no illumination among the dense, dark trees.

Martin heard girlish voices screaming behind him in loud chorus outcry.

He doubled his efforts, knowing it didn't matter if he bashed his nose again or sprained a leg, as long as he escaped here with his life.

The girls behind him shrilled with outrage that their feast was running away.

Martin stumbled, fell, pulled himself up, and emerged in a clearing on a hill.

Overhead, stars floated in a clear night sky.

Behind him were the pine trees and the vampire horde closing in. He could hear the thudding of their girlish boots on pine needles. They were getting close enough so that he could hear their grunting breaths as they sought to gain ground on him.

This was really like a scene out of a Alienopolis epic, but for real. He was the only thing close to a super hero, and he was losing ground.

Ahead of him rattled a huge, lumbering train. Thousands of tons of steel and cargo rattled past, powerful and unmindful of his helplessness:

Ker-klackker-klackkerty-klackker-klackker-klackkerty-ka-klack…

He could not get past that clattering train.

The Girl Guide vampires were almost upon him.

There is nothing quite so terrifying as having a pack of hungry, insane teenage vampire girls closing in on your back.

With a scream of terror and panic, Martin launched himself into the darkness.

By a miracle, he landed running.

He went down the hill, slightly sideways, not quite falling but no longer running. He just threw himself—with arms flailing—down the hill.

Behind him, he glimpsed a pack of running, struggling, intent, arm waving, jumping Girl Guides coming after him.

In another minute they would have him on the ground between them, and he'd be drained in seconds.

Martin ran after the train.

He saw a steel ladder, and reached for it.

His hand was roughly slammed out of the way, but his arm caught.

He contracted his body involuntarily, and stayed hooked.

The train carried him away.

The Girl Guides stood still, watching with huge black eyes and slavering fangs over red lips. Their pale faces was the last he saw of them—for the moment. He knew they would be after the train to meet him at the station and finish their little drink that little snack that Gramma had packed for them—namely, Martin.

Now he understood why Xena and Ana and the other trailer park creatures had cheered so happily at their departing scout pack.

Aching, Martin slowly climbed up the ladder. Wind rushed through his hair, rattled his clothes, and made his eyes water so that he blinked. He was glad this wasn't the old steam train scenario from black and white movies, where you had cinders flying into your eyes.

Bit by aching bit, he made his way onto a flatbed car.

There, he sank to his knees and thanked his lucky stars to be alive—so far, for however long.

The diesel engine emitted several long, barreling air horn blasts. Clearly, the train was slowing. You could feel it in the tortured squealing of the wheels and gears as the air brakes began to bite. Fifteen minutes, and it would all be over.

He could see a pair of yellowish headlights off in the distance.

Shielding his eyes from the wind, and squinting, he could make out the rental slogan on the girls' van. Lorena and Carmela must have finished their drinks in the parking lot and were racing alongside the train to catch up with him at the station ahead. Even if the train only slowed down at the station, they lived in this area and would know exactly where to wait as the train rumbled slowly past, maybe ten miles an hour at most, so they could clamber aboard and finish him off.

What to do?

Martin raised himself up on a canvas sheet covering some sort of object strapped down on the flatbed surface. There were in fact three such canvas mystery objects forming a straight line from front to back on the car's heavy wooden plank floor.

Can I hide under there?

He lifted a corner of the heavy canvas and spotted something mysterious under there. It was a motor of some type, lying on its side on a protective wooden pallet.

He saw a metal surface in the dark, and a logo: *Roto-Plexy— Fun For All.*

Curiously, he pulled the canvas further aside, and was shocked to see what he saw there.

The yellow headlights gained on the train. At about forty-five miles an hour, it was a done deal now. They would find crossing and get a few Girl Guides on board, like crazed mountain climbers in those shorts and bandannas.

Another sign read: *Easy as child's play—anyone can master Roto-Plexy in minutes.*

If this was what he hoped, he might stand a chance.

The diesel locomotives up front all blared their air horns simultaneously to warn the station master of the train's passing through.

Martin heard the alarming sound of bells slowly clanging. Alongside the tracks, red signal lights flashed over X-signs, telling the train to stop. Something up ahead—maybe a train changing tracks—required that this train come to a full stop.

You better be right. If you're wrong I'm dead.

Martin got the canvas off the gadget, even as the train slowed to a crawl

Now they were merely rolling slowly along, and not a thousand feet ahead were the flashing lights of a railroad crossing. Sitting on the street with terrifyingly glaring white headlights was the rental van full of teenage vampire Girl Guides.

Fumbling as fast as he could, Martin strapped himself into the machine.

He stood up, holding its arm rests while it hung from his shoulders. It was heavy, but just barely light enough so he could stagger forward. He flicked the control switches on a panel in front of him.

Along the tracks ahead, he could see the shadowy menacing figures of Carmela, Lorena, and the girls waiting their turn at his nectar. No telling what else the polluted waters and algae-sludge of the Salton Sea had stealthily brewed in over a century.

He must get up on top of the next canvas mound.

Up he went, clambering onto the next machine.

Already, the whirling propeller blades bit into the night air. He felt himself surrounded by a gale of furious flying dust and debris as the wings of the miniature flying machine powered up and made the titanium struts around him tremble with their power. The hybrid gasoline-diesel-propane-LNG engine roared with a steady whine like a giant model airplane.

The train slowed with screaming, grinding steel brakes like the sound of knives being sharpened.

Already, girls' clawing hands and reaching arms and black liquid eyes were visible as the troop pulled themselves up onto the train car.

Martin threw all the rocker switches onto Full Blast, and the easily controlled Child's Play Roto-Plexy personal garden flyer lifted him with a wrenching yank fifty feet off the ground before he could gain his breath back.

He was airborne—*up, up, and away!*

Chapter 10. Snow Village

To his relief, Martin was able to sit down. The Roto-Plexy Personal Flyer (R3PF) was, in some ways, a sort of flying motorcycle. Once you were airborne, you put your feet in two stirrups while sitting on a large, comfortable motorcycle seat. From the knees up, you were encased in a Plexiglas cockpit with great visibility all around.

Martin couldn't figure out how to close the bottom—maybe it didn't close; maybe this was still a prototype—so he must endure cold wind blasting his legs. From the hips up, he was inside a dimly lit cockpit illumined by a waist-level ring of faint reddish-amber light that did not interfere with night vision. There was an overhead white light, but you did not want to touch that for fear of blinding yourself.

To some extent, as he learned, this machine flew itself. It was a futuristic design—as the advertising videos inside told him in happily burbling tones—to operate on an urban network—the wired city of the future.

You had arm rests on either side with built-in controls. You had motorcycle-style handle bars, and miniature joysticks to control roll, pitch, and yaw—all the directions possible in which to fly. A nice little lap top sized display in front of the handlebars displayed real-time information.

Using tutorials, Martin taught himself to be a competent pilot. He could speak or dictate a heading based on scrolling maps, and the machine would keep itself level and fly in whatever direction you told it to. It stayed on average about five hundred feet above ground level, controlled by the CPU.

Martin frantically wanted to get away from the State 84 and I-10 corridor and thus avoid any chance of the vampire teenage girls pursuing him.

He studied the maps and decided his next best bet was to follow something called the Pacific Crest Trail. No van, nor any form of automobile, could possibly follow him along that winding dirt hiking path up and down mountain trails. He'd never actually seen this great hiking path, but it ran over 2,600 miles (over 4,000 km) from the US-Mexican border at Campo, near San Diego, to the US-Canadian border at Manning Park, British Columbia. The trail cut through twenty-five U.S. national forests and seven national parks. Elevations ranged from near sea level in some areas to over two miles high in the Sierra Nevada in the north. Along that route, it would pass through some tall mountains in southern California.

As best Martin could figure, if he told the R3PF's guidance system to follow this trail, it would take him as far north as he needed to go before heading west to LA. Traveling at a nice clip of about sixty miles per hour, he would reach the San Bernardino area by dawn.

As the plane hummed happily along, Martin studied the maps and refined his travel plan. He verbally instructed the guidance system to change course for San Bernardino, which would be a slightly westward veer from around Palm Springs.

With a sinking feeling, he saw a warning notice: *Fuel Advisement.*

"Oh no, now what?" He exclaimed. His voice triggered a response from the R3PF. A breathy, almost drunken sounding, lush female voice said, "This is your trip advisor, urgently suggesting route alternatives. Your fuel is running low."

Martin said, "Voice, what is fuel status?"

"Fuel status is low. You will run out of fuel at present altitude and vector in between thirty and forty minutes."

"Can I get as far as San Bernardino?"

"You can get within fifty miles if you stay on present course."

"Is that the optimum?"

"That is optimum considering all factors including velocity, elevation, and air quality."

"Then keep me going as far as possible."

Martin studied the fuel supply situation next. The machine only took a very specific type of fuel that had been carried with the demo models on the train. It was not available publicly, and the system warned him that the engine could explode if he put in any other sort of fuel, including gasoline, diesel, or natural gas.

"Houston, we have ourselves an *aw shit.*"

Houston did not reply, because he was in a new world nobody had ever explored or even heard of.

So he prepared himself for the worst.

He tracked the onboard monitoring systems as the Pacific Crest Trail wandered northward. His legs started to become cold and numb as the trail gradually rose higher and higher in the San Jacinto Mountain area east of Los Angeles.

Now—at last, if nothing else—he saw the words *Los Angeles* on the monitor for the first time. If only this blasted machine had a wrap-around cockpit. He found a heater, and turned it on full blast, which kept him warm to just below the knees. He squirmed until he was sitting on the backrest of the seat, with his feet on the motorcycle seat itself.

If he got through this alive, he would certainly send a customer service letter to the makers of the R3PF. *Wonderful gadget—needs work.*

A warning buzzer sounded, followed by the lush, breathy woman's voice.

"Alert. Altitude. You are crossing over half a mile altitude and continuing to rise."

"Hello? Hello?" Martin called out. "You told me to fly straight."

A male voice cut in, "Deviation will cost fuel. Stay on course."

Martin watched helplessly as the ground rose ahead of him.

From the maps, he could see that he was heading into a complex of mountains including the Santa Rosas of Southern California and the San Jacinto National Park area of the Peninsular Mountain Ranges. It was a complex, confusing picture.

Now he had both the male and female robot voices talking to him at cross-purposes, while a red warning light began to flash and a legend appeared: *Running Low on Fuel.*

Other warnings began to tell of outside temperatures dropping below freezing.

As he flew higher, the air outside was drier and colder. It was costing more fuel to fly. At the same time, he must stay on a straight course to conserve his remaining fuel. The glassy cockpit window was starting to ice over on the outside, and fog up on the inside. He had the blower on max, and there was nothing else he could do. The machine was flying itself, the warnings said he had ten minutes' flight time left, and he had no idea where he was.

The last indicator said that he was within San Jacinto State Park an hour's drive west of Palm Springs—assuming there was a straight road, which there wasn't. It was all mountain peaks, some of them more than two miles in altitude and covered with snow. The northern face of San Jacinto Peak was one of the highest in the continental United States.

Martin's frantic studies were cut short when the R3PF began

making shuddering noises.

"Emergency descent," said the male and female voices in unison. "Emergency descent. Brace for impact. Brace for impact."

"Air temperature is thirty degrees and falling."

Martin climbed as high on the seat as he could, held out his arms in either direction, with his palms splayed to brace himself, and closed his eyes.

Had he been counting, he estimated, it would have been less than sixty seconds to impact.

The cockpit shielded him from the worst effects, though the Plexiglas cracked and split in several directions. The craft fell over onto one side. One stirrup had been bent backward, and the other was smashed.

As he crawled out from under the wreckage, he noted the broken rotors and knew this poor craft would never fly again. Worse yet, he was dressed only in a sweatsuit, with cowboy boots and no socks. Instantly, as he crawled out from the smashed aircraft, he was in six inches of snow, with his body temperature in danger of dropping to deadly depths.

He rose, hopping about and banging his hands together. If only he had gloves.

If only, if only!

If a hesitant twilight had been growing in the cockpit's frosty window, it was now dawn as Martin stood looking about. Far off in the freezing cold distance, across miles and miles of empty air, he saw a golden glow tinged with pink on the craggy teeth of remote mountain peaks.

He stood at an intersection in some sort of alpine village. Immediately around him were stone buildings, all of which looked buttoned up and uninhabited. The cross streets were narrow and led away into deep alpine forests. He saw some electrical cables overhead, but something—a lightning strike maybe—had struck the main trans box and torn it open, blackening it, so that frayed ends of severed wires and cables hung uselessly out.

He took out the cell phone and tried that. Again, he had a recorded, downloaded message from Chloë,

> Oh Martin starting to
> despair am so
> disappointed

And there it cut off, with no punctuation, no sense of what she meant.

Once again, he tried calling out, and once again his phone interpreted the problem for him—

> No out signal

He tried texting her, but the signal was dead.

"Oh my god," he cried. "Chloë, have faith in me, baby. You are all I have to live for. I would be dead without you." He sank to his knees in the snow and sobbed. "I am all alone. I have nobody. I am nobody. I am nothing. Oh god, oh Chloë, are you even real, baby? Did I dream you up? Have I ever lived in San Diego? Do I have a pesty sister named Nancy or is that also a hideous nightmare beyond comprehension? Mom? Dad? I'm sorry. I love you."

He looked at the dead phone.

"Over," he said sadly, "and out."

He looked at the phone for a moment, wanting to throw it as far as he could, but resisted the temptation. Instead, he slipped it back into his hoodie pocket.

Freezing, he rose and staggered down the street. He caught a glimpse of himself in a window: haggard, horrified, humble, harpsichord. Anything beginning with H as in Hell. Or heck, if one was a prude, but then again even churches must be suspect. Where was Al-Balaam when you needed him? Nix, nada, no signal. Does not compute. Does not exist. It's all a scam to sell marijuana to stupid people and be zillionaires who own the skyline.

Sniffling, he shuffled down the street in his cowboy boots.

He came to a roadblock covered with snow. The red and white striped barrier must have been here for a long time. A sign read, *Road Closed.*

A sign overhead read, *Jacinto City, Pop. 40. Closed for Season. See you back soon! (happy face).*

What did that mean? It was summer—so what season? Oh yes, maybe it was a ski resort, closed temporarily.

He wandered back to the intersection. The whole town was only a few hundred feet across.

By the burned out transformer was a sign, *Power out until Season. Emergency Backup Only.*

The lower half of that sign had been burned and singed, not by human intention, so it must be that even emergency power had been knocked out here in Jacinto City.

He walked along the two main (and only) cross streets. He needed to get inside somehow, maybe burn logs or something, and look for a way to call out for help. This was a state park, so there must be California Forest Service fire watch or state park rangers someplace. How to reach them was the question. How to get warm and prevent death by cold was the more pressing issue.

A small section of one street had actual, honest to goodness store windows—presumably for the tourist season. People came here, ate ice cream, spent the night, sent cards home, and shopped.

One store window had mannequins in it. Now that looked like a shopping hot spot. A bare display with two and a half female mannequins. One was missing her upper half, just a pair of legs on a stand. One wore a dress and a flowery hat. The other was bald and stark naked.

"Ladies," he chided, while using a large rock to smash the window.

Hoping to hear a burglar alarm, he stopped and listened.

All he heard was freezing wind keening on the snowy slopes around the mountain peak.

He climbed in through the broken window into what felt like a refrigerator. At least there was not that persistent, cruel, horrifying wind. Just a kind of mortuary chill that settled into your bones.

He kicked the back wall out of the display and stepped into a small gift shop.

It was gloomy inside. Several male and female mannequins sporting fun wear looked frozen and bizarre. One held up a warning finger. Two of them were so lifelike and seemed to be tracking him with their eyes that Martin got goose bumps. One of them scared him so much that he kicked it over. It was a male figure wearing a flowery shirt, shorts, a nice pair of crew socks, and hiking boots. It landed face down and lay still.

Martin sat down beside it, pulled off his boots, and untied its shoes. Pulling the shoes off—one of the feet broke away—he managed to get the socks off and—something.

He leaned in for a close sniff. The shoes had a funny, faintly decayed smell.

Not a rotting corpse smell or anything; just this odd, dirty-socks odor.

Whatever. They would help him keep warm and survive.

He pulled the socks on, and the cowboy boots back over those.

He felt better already. He looked around. Oh lordy, hallelujah— he saw a nice ski parka. It was purple as a grape, and had nice down cross-stitched inside. Gratefully, he slipped it on. It was light and warm. Now he was in business. He ransacked the store, looking for other goodies. He found matches, lighters, and a little propane stove for campers.

Yeah, this is the ticket.

He found an oil lantern and lit it carefully, replacing the glass chimney to prevent fire. He didn't know how long he must survive here, so best to preserve his advantages.

The place did give him the creeps.

He took all the mannequins and moved them to the front window.

They still gave him the creeps with their stiff gestures and staring eyes.

So he threw them out the window, making a pile in the street.

Back in the store, he looked at all the power lines. Everything was dead. Must have been a lightning strike that knocked out the transformers. Or sometimes you read that a squirrel gnawed though a cable, got itself fried while short-circuiting some key wires, and bingo, the power was out for miles around.

As a good thing, he found some military-style MREs (Meals Ready to Eat) to go with his little portable stove.

Groaning with some relief, he stomped up a spiral staircase to reach the building's upper story.

There, he was in an empty room about forty by forty feet—a

storage unit, emptied before its abandonment. Something told him nobody would be returning here for weeks, if not months, when the owners of this place (the *evil gummint* of paranoid fantasies?) would start preparing for fall ski season.

It would not do to try and light this little gas-powered camping stove inside the building. *Maybe up on the roof, eh?* He climbed up a wooden stairway to a platform at the top. A fire door led from that outside onto a tarpaper and leaded roof.

Icy cold and grit flew into his face. His cheeks stung with ice crystals hurled about. The wind had a low, moaning, keening sound.

There was a wall about three feet high made of lumber sheathed with roofing materials. This blocked the worst of the cold wind. Several places had steel plates lying presumably over ceiling windows that were closed up for winter. Martin picked the most sheltered of these plates to start his camp stove. He opened a beef and macaroni dinner, whose metallic saucer he placed over the gas. Sorting through the box, he laid aside plastic fork, spoon, and knife as well as little plastic sacks of ketchup, Parmesan cheese, and other condiments.

He felt better. At least he could survive long enough to hatch up a Plan B.

The mac 'n beef wasn't bad. It filled him up, warmed him, and made him wish for a nice hot cup of coffee. *Oops*—he could figure something out for that as well. He collected a tin cup of snow melt from the topmost roof area. He heated the weater until it began to boil. He'd found packets of coffee, creamer, and sugar, and put in just enough to his own sparse taste. He liked his coffee dark but not black, with just a hint of sweetness but mainly bite. That accomplished, in the manner of a Robinson Crusoe—he gripped his coffee. Sipping the hot liquid gingerly, he walked around his domain.

He looked out at the distant mountains, which had begun to glow a sort of lemon-yellow and then orange juice as full daylight crept over the snow fields and crevices.

In the distance to the west, he saw a passenger jet cruising by. Ah yes, of course, the great airport at LAX. Actually, it was a city of airports, so it could be LAX or any number of other air fields. Good deal. He was within viewing distance of civilization. Maybe as daylight fully set in, he'd be able to glimpse the skyline.

Oh god yes and Chloë is there waiting for me. I'm coming, sweetheart. I'm on the way, darling!

Around him, the tiny city of Jacinto glowered cold and dead as a cemetery.

It was spooky, actually.

No lights inside, no life—just darkness like a mausoleum.

As the wind shifted, for the first time he detected an odd, unpleasant smell.

It was a bit like the smell in the mannequin's socks.

He rumpled his nose and began to feel worried.

Was that a noise, or just the wind?

He heard a tinkling sound.

A kind of shuffling.

Maybe a sob.

Walking around the roof, he looked down on each side.

He saw the brick walls, other walls of gray granite. He saw lead sheathing, roofing material, ice flowing down the walls outside, snow layered on every flat surface.

And that wind kept keening and moaning all around.

He looked down into the street, seeing the crashed R3PF flyer in the middle of the intersection. The street in both directions was covered with virgin snow. Only his own tracks disturbed it, leading from the crashed plane to the window of the building he was in.

Leaning out a bit, he looked down to see the pile of mannequins he had thrown out the window.

They were all gone.

He dropped his cup, which sailed end over end, spilling coffee, and landed in the snow.

Where had they gone? Who had taken them? And why?

This could not mean anything good.

There was a trail in the snow, leading along the side of the building. Someone had come sneaking alongside the building, picked up the dead mannequins, and carried them away.

Why on earth would anyone do such a thing?

Only if they were stark raving mad. A lunatic.

Another Marsha Stark and Josie Klein combination, maybe.

Suddenly shot through with terror, he hurried to the door he'd come out of.

Must stop, must listen.

He heard nothing except the wind.

One room at a time. He must get back to the main floor.

Down the stairs he went.

His breath sawed across his ribs, painfully, as his heart wildly beat.

Then, halfway down the stairs into the main store, he froze.

What?

Across the street—figures.

Zombie mannequins.

They had gathered in a dark place, it was immediately apparent to Martin. What else could it be?

Impossible, but there they are.

Maybe someone was animating these things. That must be it.

Reality: deal with reality.

Were they remote-robots? Could there really be an evil gummint? Were the paranoid nuts watching false news right after all? Were their fake views and button-pushing mob-control messages somehow founded in fact?

As he stared with stomach acid rising up his esophagus, he recognized the male whose foot had come off. The thing hopped toward him on one foot, supporting itself by a hand on the shoulder of a female that wore only a bra and a half-slip. The female looked almost elegant as she (it) strode forward with its hands curving and its fingers delicately angled.

Nearby came a pair of female legs with no torso or head.

There must be ten or fifteen of these things. A few carried objects, including one with a fire axe that looked like it (he) meant business.

Martin ran down the rest of the steps and fumbled at the door. He was so cared and nervous that his hands did not seem to grip. He flailed helplessly but got the fire bar locked on the door, meaning it was locked inwardly and outwardly—he hoped.

He remembered with regret having broken through the window display.

A glance into the street revealed that they were halfway across. More zombie mannequins were joining them from all directions.

Martin threw whatever objects he could find through the broken wall, in hope of plugging up the entry he'd made. If nothing else, it might slow them down.

He must have a longer-term strategy, but right now it was a matter of surviving from one minute to the next. He piled sleeping bags, books, backpacks, gas canisters, cooking stoves, MRE packages, boxes of shoes and boots—anything he could find—to plug the hole.

Now he heard them at the door.

Fumbling.

He could see through the window panes—vague, blank looks.

He saw the fire axe rise, counted two seconds while it fell, and heard the resounding smash as it hit the door. But the door held. Thank god.

As they pounded and pulled at the door, Martin frantically ransacked the store looking for weapons. He did find a large knife, which he tucked into his waistband. He also found a box of road flares, which he dropped into a small backpack. He threw the knife in there as well.

The nagging worry was that, if he set the building on fire with the flares—might he burn to death along with these zombie things?

Under a chair, he found the foot he had severed from the shoe zombie.

He picked it up, examined it, half expected to see gears and wheels inside.

Nothing. Hollow.

These were not robots. They were spirits. Ghosts. It wasn't the evil gummint. It was fate, karma, kismet, whatever you wanted to call it. He, Martin Brown, must have the worst whatchamacallit in history.

He heard a groan, a sob, a sniffle.

They were at the window now. Stupid as they were, they had figured out that the door was too hard. They had sought and found the next best entrance point—the same window by which Martin had entered. Maybe there was some faint glimmer of zombie memory. The mannequins who had been in the window remembered their long-time perch and communicated its location to their fellow idiots.

The piled backpacks, sleeping bags, shopping bags, gift packs, teddy bears, MREs and so forth began to move. First a plaster hand appeared, then a chipped, vacant face topped with waves of brown painted hair. Then the shoulders of a male zombie wiggled in.

Martin found a claw hammer and smashed its head in.

As he wielded the hammer—as its steel claws bit into the empty cranium of the mannequin—a hand gripped the hammer.

Martin pulled his hand away, feeling stung. He'd felt a cold, hard plaster hand against his own.

Now a male zombie had the hammer—holding it, and looking

at him. Its face was expressionles but seemed to radiate that the tables were turned.

Martin overturned a clothing rack with purses and ladies' dresses onto it.

The zombie was briefly tangled.

Martin took the opportunity to run back up the stairs.

There was nothing up there to block the stairs—the storage floor was empty.

He was trapped, and they were going to kill him.

No time now to ask why—time to act. Run! But how, and where to?

He emerged on the roof, carrying his backpack with flares and knife.

These creatures would take the knife from him, moving however slowly like sloths, and kill him with it.

He could not even lock the roof door from outside.

He heard them shuffling on the stairs.

In a moment they'd be on the roof.

He looked frantically down—two or three stories onto a concrete sidewalk. If he jumped, he'd be either dead or crippled.

As he circled on the roof, he spotted a long wooden ladder. It was splintered and weathered, but long enough to reach the next rooftop.

He threw it across, just as the first shuffling figures appeared on the roof.

The one with the fire axe was now the leader.

Martin climbed on the ladder, shakily, and spread his arms like a tightrope walker.

He ran across to the other building and just made it as the ladder slipped and went crashing down into an alley below. He heard it bounce and crash among trash cans and steel dumpsters.

The zombies stood on the roof across from him. They looked blankly in his direction. A few looked downward. Looking across in sick fascination, he saw the woman-legs thing running around in circles. Its stop-go body motions suggested it was able to look this way or that, up or down.

He turned and looked about. The roof here was as empty as the one he'd come from. There was a doorway in a sort of shed structure, similar to the stairwell on the other side.

With his elbow, he broke a glass pane. Carefully reaching in—

hoping the place did not have its own mannequins—he found a door handle and twisted.

A clicking sound told him the door was unlocked now. He pulled it open, stepped inside, and pulled it shut. It did not lock.

Inside was darkness. This was another upper-story storage area like the empty one on the other side, only this one was stocked with many dark shapes.

His heart beat wildly. What if it was full of mannequins? What if they'd herded him here to finish him off?

He saw what looked like canvas-covered boxes. Not a single R3PF among them, sadly. Mostly gifts for the spring tourist season, he imagined.

He bolted down the stairs, past the second floor which was shrouded in darkness, and into the street-level shop. Light fell in, gray and indistinct, but enough to see by. The doors and windows were intact. How long would it take these zombies to figure out how to reach him?

Only a matter of time—not much of it, at that.

A sign above the counter read: Hansen's Sporting Goods.

He searched through the backpacks, ski poles, skis, binoculars, anything a person would want—except something like a six-gauge, single-barrel shotgun with rounds of heavy shot to spray these monstrous creatures all over the place.

As he frantically searched about, he heard shuffling noises. Through a store window, he spotted the mannequin with the fire axe standing outside. With it were other mannequins including females. They had armed themselves with hammers, tire irons, and steel rods. They were getting stronger.

Meaner and more determined.

Desperately, Martin looked around, until he saw on the wall what his terrified eyes had failed to see.

On the wall in one section were gliders.

He scrambled forward and pulled a demo off the wall.

It was a hang glider with its wings folded for storage in a car.

He recognized them from years of seeing people fly them off the cliffs at Torrey Pines in San Diego. He was running out of options. This was now his only hope.

He stuck a flare in each pocket for good measure. He dropped his backpack, abandoning his weapons. That allowed him to concentrate on the most important task—manhandling the light but unwieldy hang glider up the stairs. It would be his only possible ticket out of this place.

As he did so, the fire axe crashed through the door.

Immediately, the air filled with a frenzy of splintering and smashing as the fire axe was followed by hammers, steel bars, even a metal camping stool.

The legs-only female came dashing inside.

It looked left, right, then fastened on him and ran up the stairs toward him.

He kicked it backward, and it went sailing through the air.

He did not stop to look where it landed, but hurried up the stairs with his glider.

Out on the roof, he despaired.

Could he get it unfolded?

Patience, this is a simple thing.

With fumbling trembling fingers, he got the struts out—unfolded, and locked outward.

He heard the shuffling of zombie feet coming up the stairs not ten feet behind him.

With the harness buckled around himself, he closed his eyes, prayed, and launched off the third story roof—to his death, or to continued life.

He heard one last crashing sound behind him.

The hang glider caught a breeze.

For a moment, he thought he was going to turn sideways and knife-edge to a horrible smashing death. Instead, swinging his feet in the direction of the slip, he righted the glider.

Then—*o miracle!*—a wind caught it from underneath and propelled him away from the roof, away from the buildings, away from the intersection, and out over empty air.

He was sailing over a thousand-foot cliff overlooking angry black crags and white angel-wings of ice.

He felt like a fly over a lake—tiny, living from second to second, but surviving.

He caught an updraft, and sailed in a long, fast arc past pink and golden snow fields basking in morning sunlight from the east.

The air grew thicker and warmer as he descended.

His legs, with their cowboy boots, hung downward as he gripped the control handles and taught himself the basic maneuvers for flying. All he wanted to do now was get down near sea level. He was a mile and a half up, by his estimation, which was terrifying but also gave him some leeway for failure—as long as he did not run face first into a cliff, nor slip on a cold draft and plummet thousands of feet to his death.

Bit by bit, he felt himself getting lower to the earth.

Tree tops flew by underneath.

Wind howled around him.

He was cold.

His worst fear now was crash landing. He must figure out how to pilot this thing down to a survivable landing.

Or die in a horrible crash.

Chapter 11. Evil Gummint

As he descended to the desert floor, Martin began to be buffeted by hot updrafts. He tried swinging gently this way and that, and was terrified at the exaggerated effects of every motion. What to do now?

He spotted birds in the air—big ones higher up, like hawks; smaller ones in greater numbers below him.

He saw a road below, some buildings, trucks parked with their windshields blazing with desert sunlight.

He heard a tiny popping noise, and then another, followed by a peppering of pops.

Someone was shooting at him.

Oh god what now?

He looked up and saw a tiny tear in the nylon above his head.

Abruptly, suicidally, he twisted himself about, aiming the glider in a desperate corkscrew turn that rapidly took him away from where he had been shot at.

It was fifty-fifty, he figured. He would either fly toward the shooter, or away.

The popping sounds grew fainter and stopped.

He looked down for signs of human motion, but saw none. The trucks stayed parked.

At that moment, his cell phone made a toilet-flushing sound.

He answered on speaker phone. "Hello?"

"Oh, Martin," came a broken voice.

"Chloë! I'm on my way to you."

"I am so disappointed."

"Chloë, I am still on my way."

"And I trusted you so much."

"Chloë—whatever you're thinking, I can explain."

She said sadly: "I had a call from the bank here in LA, saying that a Martin Brown hacked into our account and tried to steal ten thousand dollars. How could you?"

"Chloë, my wallet was stolen."

She was silent.

"Chloë, I am all in the air over you right now. I mean literally. I am somewhere over Riverside, hang gliding down to the desert. I'll tell you all about it when I see you. I did not hack your account."

She said, "Oh, Martin," and then the phone went dead.

"Chloë?"

Sadly, he slipped the phone back into his hoodie pocket.

So that was over now.

Gone.

No interview, no Chloë. No love, no life, no hope.

What would Maritza Dusenbery say?

Would Carol Monegan ever speak to him again?

Would Alicia Washington ever regain faith in him?

Would the guys shun him? Would his sister Nancy sneer all the more?

Would Mom and Dad shake their heads mournfully?

He could see the horrific ripple effects of his last disastrous—what had it been?—twelve hours?

In barely half a day, his life had been ruined.

He thought back. Dusk had just begun setting over San Diego as he had left for points north. It should have been a simple two-hour drive. He and Chloë could be in love and maybe engaged to be married by now. Maybe in an alternate universe. Not in this one run by Al-Balaam and his chorus of marijuana-growing demons in choir robes.

Martin began to boil over with rage.

Enough was enough.

He'd had it.

I'm damned mad, and I'm not going to take this anymore.

Someone was shooting at him, and that was the last straw.

Why wasn't he more tired? He remembered the ginseng tea those witches at Bombay Beach had given him the night before. Must have been some diluted, long-term meth in there or something.

He must be down to about 1,000 feet now and cruising nicely in circles.

He saw a road below, deserted in both directions from horizon to horizon.

Other than that, he saw some sand dunes and maybe a little oasis with some cactus and Joshua trees. Best to steer in that direction. He might be the midst of one of the world's most uninhabitable deserts and use some water and shade. Then he could think about his next move—assuming nobody shot at him again.

He sailed in low over sandrock and scrubby hills. Nice place to land there in the middle of that dune. He swung his feet forward to tilt the glider's front wing edge up a trifle. He could feel his fall slowing—a controlled fall.

He came in a bit too fast—braked with a forward swing—and crashed, rolling, into hard sand like broken glass.

He was shaken up, but he was on the ground and alive.

For a moment, he lay on the sand. He felt stunned and winded. *Nothing broken.*

Rattled but intact, he sat up. The glider lay crumpled around him. It would never fly again either, shades of the R3PF.

He unstrapped himself, rolled over, and stood up.

He was shaky for a moment, but regained his composure.

What now?

It was morning, and the sun was a hot yellow ball over *there*, so *there* must be east. Then the opposite must be west, in that direction, and that was how he'd go.

He started walking.

Oh god it was hot.

He stopped to peel off his hoodie, and the sweat pants from Bombay Beach. From what he'd heard, the desert got cold at night—nothing to hold the heat in; the sand mostly deflected sunlight; so the heat rose and blew away, leaving the door open for chilly wind to flow in like refrigerated water in the night. He hoped not to be anywhere near here by night, but you never knew.

He made a bundle of the sweatsuit, leaving one sleeve out for a carrying strap, and swung it over his shoulder. A minute later, he eased the heat in his boots by removing the zombie socks and leaving them in the sand. His feet had a vague mortuary smell, but that would wash away with sweat. He wanted to keep the boots off, but the sand was too hot and glassy.

As he walked, he had a vague sense of going toward that oasis he'd seen from the air. That would be perfect for the moment.

He was also conscious that he was wearing nothing but underpants and boots. He didn't even have socks or a T-shirt now. The sun would broil him like a lobster unless he found a solution.

That solution came barely a few minutes later.

As he hiked across the hard sand, he avoided slopes upward or downward to conserve energy. Instead, he kept to the median altitudes and walked almost level. Like so much of this vast southwestern desert complex, this was ground near sea level. Millions of years ago, this had all been underwater. He was walking on the bed of a primordial sea. In these shallow waters—eons ago—dinosaurs, and giant lizards, and prehistoric sharks the size of moving vans had fought to the death for survival.

He spotted an odd sort of scraggle or squiggle of unnatural color about two hundred feet ahead.

As he drew near, walking at a steady pace, he suspected the worst.

And he was right.

The object half buried in the sand was a dead man.

He stopped and looked down at this sad relic.

What could this have been all about?

He squatted down and inspected the death spot.

He saw a skull that had been there for some time. It wasn't totally bleached, but still had yellowish fatty sediments of flesh printed on its surfaces. This guy had probably been alive a year or two ago. The face lay in the sand with a big grin, staring up through hollow eyes. As Martin poked it with his finger, a lizard flowed out and ran off in a flash.

Behind the skull lay a helmet—a sky diver's helmet, still buckled with a frayed leather chin strap. Not government issue, but a sporting type; purple.

The body was mostly buried in sand, both from impact and wind drift. Martin decided to look for some identification, in case he should make it to civilization and send searchers this way. Why a purple helmet?

Gradually, he unearthed a dark-green jump suit. Bones fell out, clattering, as he lifted the suit. It had large yellow buttons up and down the front. How odd. And some nice boots. This had been a big man. Martin wondered if the boots would fit him. Size twelve—too big. Best stick with the smelly cowboy boots. But there were some olive-green military type socks. Happily, Martin slipped those over his feet. *Beggars can't be choosers.* The military socks were big, but they'd fit in the cowboy boots.

If the guy had a 'shute, it had blown away long ago. He had the full harness—and, o lordie, an assault rifle. Now what did that mean? A sporting jumper with an assault rifle. He had a belt with extra rounds, and a canteen whose water had evaporated from under the screw top lid. Martin found a belt pack with a booklet in it, titled *Government is not the solution. Government is the problem.*

Martin had a film enthusiast's nodding familiarity with weapons. The assault rifle had gotten tangled in the man's clothing, and probably was still well enough oiled to function. The ammo looked dry and should work. Ah, there was a web belt with a 9 millimeter automatic and several clips. And a very nice, all-purpose Ranger knife with a black, matte handle, in a dark green sheath and not at all rusty. The dry climate out here would have seen to that. No radio, orders, or other information. In the belt pack were the mummified remains of a sandwich, an apple, and a candy bar.

Martin put the man's T-shirt on himself. It felt dry and might crumble, but it was better than getting baked by the sun. Also, the man had a dark blue baseball cap tucked into a shoulder epaulet, which Martin put on his own head. The cap was unfortunately decorated with a home-made device that told much about its owner— an eagle gripping a globe with its talons, surrounded by laurels, with a swastika carved into the globe. Maybe a militia enthusiast out on maneuvers, who met an unforeseen end and was never found by his fellow neo-Nazis. The cap would help Martin survive out here, but he would throw it away before anyone could see him wearing it.

He left the man's jumpsuit spread-eagled on the sand— weighted down with the canteen and helmet. He noticed two labels on the chest. On the wearer's left side was a name tag—*Jones*—and on the right side of his chest over the pocket was the legend *Freedom Defense Force.*

He took the weapons and ammo along—on a hunch. Someone had been shooting at him. That might just require a defensive posture.

Defenders of Freedom Fries, Martin thought. *What a waste.*

Hiking on, Martin came to a low area with a dry wash. No water. There were some hardy desert plants, which maybe relied on the occasional night dew or even more occasional rain sprinkle for survival. A small gray lizard looked at him, flicked its tongue to taste the air, and vanished in one motion.

Near the head of the wash he did find a metal sign on a desiccated wooden four-by-four post. Written in black letters on white enamel background were the words: *Federal Government Property. Top Secret Defense Department Installation. No Trespassing. Danger of Sentries Shooting If Intruder Shows Weapons. Surrender at Main Gate.*

This was followed by some lettering in small print about U.S. Code this or that.

Martin removed the Nazi baseball cap and scratched his head. He had put on the web gear, which was made heavy by the automatic and ammo. He carried the M-16 looped over his shoulder, but considered jettisoning it. He wished he had a radio, or even a signaling mirror to end this nightmare by being found. He did not want to be shot for brandishing weapons, but someone had been shooting at him. Who would do that?

What was this place? And why?

If only he knew where the main gate was—he'd gladly surrender.

As he marched on across the empty desert, which was relieved only by low, stunted vegetation, Martin began to suffer from dehydration.

Every gust of hot wind peppered him with grit, very much like sandpaper.

He could feel himself growing light-headed under the neo-Nazi baseball cap. If only he had some salt tablets. More than anything, he daydreamed about a large pitcher of cold orange juice from a nice refrigerator at—yes, horrors—mom and dad's house. Nancy would hug him, hold him, feed him cold cuts with mustard or something, maybe something to really make the kid in him barf—olive and pimiento loaf in bologna—but make him feel at home.

Oh to be home again! Now more than ever it looked as if he'd never make it. Every year, untold numbers of people died in these Southwestern deserts. Some, like the late paratrooper, would not be found for years—if ever. He thought about making one last call to Chloë, telling her goodbye—but he could not bear the thought of hearing his misunderstanding and disappointed voice again. He would rather die remembering her as things had been just two days ago—new love, fresh as creation, lovely as dawn; sunny and fragrant, among the finest moments life had to offer any person.

Lost in thought, Martin kept on walking.

Then, *something*—he heard voices.

Am I dreaming?

He dropped to his belly.

There, he heard men talking.

He rubbed his eyes and tried to think clearly. Carefully sitting up, he looked around—and spotted a vehicle nearby. It was one of those quasi-military vehicles, maybe a Hummer, painted in pink and mauve camouflage stripes, with clown faces painted on its sides. How odd was that?

The vehicle baked in the sun beside a sand dune. There was no shade out here, but someone had at least parked in the shelter of a dune and away from the biting, hot wind.

Could these be the people who had shot at him while he was gliding down?

He held the M-16 before him in both hands and inched forward on his elbows in a high crawl.

The voices came from his right somewhere. Two men, talking, who did not seem perturbed.

The car was more on his left, ahead, and he crawled toward that.

It had civilian plates from Nevada. It had a black ragtop and open windows on all sides. He could see inside—it was deserted.

He looked around and saw nobody watching the car. Now at a run, he approached the vehicle.

He saw maps, oranges, a water bottle—he tore the top off and drank deeply.

Nobody said anything.

Couple of crackers and some cheese—salt never tasted so good.

He held the rifle before him and advanced toward the voices.

He found two men crouched behind a ridge.

On closer examination, they were not only men but clowns.

Circus clowns. Each man wore a gray conical hat festooned with
yellow and pink paper chrysanthemums and a bright blue fluffy ball
on the peak. They wore fatigue uniforms with zebra striping in
subdued cream, pink, dark gray, and mauve colors like their vehicle.
Each had a white Elizabethan collar that spread out like a disk over
his neck.

One was just looking at a map spread before him. The other
scanned the horizon with binoculars. Each had an assault rifle lying
to one side. Each had a black sidearm in a green military-style holster
dangling from a web belt.

The click made by Martin putting his rifle on rock and roll made
them whirl.

"You touch the weapons, you're dead," Martin said. "I am
beyond letting anyone fuck with me."

"Now see here," said the older, a gray-haired clown.

"No, you see here," Martin said. "Start talking. Who are you?
If you fuck with me, I'll kill you. Was that you assholes shooting at
me?"

The younger man, skinny, about thirty, with lank, curly black
hair, looked upset. "I'm sorry. We thought you were a government
man."

"I am your worst nightmare right now," Martin said. "You put
a bullet through my wing. I could put a round through your clown
suit."

The older man looked sick. "I'm sorry. We are looking for a
missing man."

"Jones?"

They both looked shocked. "You know Benny?"

"Benny is dead."

The older man started to cry. "He was my son-in-law."

"Right, and I am a Yeti." Martin was moved by the man's tears.
"What are a pair of clowns doing here? Where is the circus?"

"The circus is the movement," the elder man said. "Freedom is
the game."

The younger man said, "Look, we'll level. I'm Stan Belkin.
This is my uncle, Steve Lowicki. We belong to a militia group. We
are wearing disguises in case the evil gummint-types catch us. We'll
say we are with a traveling circus and we got lost."

"Armed to the teeth," Martin said acidly. "Nuts." Their faces
had faint traces of white makeup and clown paint that had sweated

away in trails of chalk and mascara in this heat.

Stan admitted "Yes, we hate the government. Yes, we want to save America from liberals, progressives, aliens, traitors, foreign socialists, inferior races, and devil-worshipers..." He paused for breath. "I could go on. But we aren't here to wage war. We are on a recovery mission. We've been afraid Benny Jones is dead. We wanted to bring his body back to his wife Mary. That's Steve's daughter."

"And you thought shooting at an unarmed paraglider would help you find Jones. What kind of complete assholes are you? Oh never mind, you've already explained how stupid two dupes can be. Excellent disguise, guys. I would never have figured you are clowns."

"Easy, mister," said the older man. "We're in the desert here in hostile territory."

"The U.S. Government."

"Your government, not ours."

"Spare me the oxygen. Look, you assholes, I want to get out of here alive. You want the bones of Benny Jones, right?"

They nodded.

"You have a vehicle. I don't. I don't want to leave you out here to die. So let's make a deal."

"We're game," Steve said with gritted teeth and defeated eyes.

"We'll go get the bones. You take him home. You get me out of here. I'm just a guy who got lost and is trying to get to Los Angeles."

They looked at each other, nodded, and said, "It's a deal. Thank you."

Martin rose and held the rifle on them. "Let's begin with you two walking toward the car. Leave the arsenal here. Drop your sidearms, too."

They looked distressed.

"Drop 'em!"

Reluctantly, as if being forced to leave part of their identities in the sand, they undid their belts and dropped the weapons. Hopefully Martin thought, they were both now actually unarmed—no hidden bazookas or nuclear bombs. That gave him an advantage if they tried anything. "Let's go. There's not much time. Can you find your way out of here?"

Steve gave him a crafty look. "We've found our way in here

several times without being noticed by the jackbooted thugs. We can get in and out."

"Good. Pick up the remains, get me out of here, and we'll go our separate ways."

"If the goons attack we'll be defenseless."

"If you stayed home, working at a day job like normal people, you wouldn't need to worry about things like that."

"You don't understand," Stan Belkin said.

"I don't want to."

They trudged toward the Hummer. Stan told Martin, "You should listen to Steve."

Martin shouldered the M-16, but kept his pistol on them. "Just focus on what we need to do."

"You know this is a federal base," Steve said. "A top secret one."

"I read the sign."

"You don't know what goes on here."

"We're not supposed to."

"Right," said Stan. "And you believe in Santa Claus."

"What's that supposed to mean?"

"Aliens."

The two clowns nodded eagerly.

"Oh my aching lord."

"No, really. We've seen them."

Martin laughed tiredly. "You mean like Area 51."

Steve snorted. "That's a blind. This here's the real thing."

Martin laughed again. "Area what? What's the name of this base?"

"Area Null," Stan said. He wasn't laughing.

"We don't have time for this bullshit." They reached the car, and the two prisoners waited for instructions.

"You guys sit in front. I'll sit in back with this piece aimed at you. You mess with me, I pop you. I'll apologize beforehand, but you shot at me first and tried to kill me."

"That was the fog of war," Steve said. "We are now your prisoners."

"You sound like robots," Martin said. "Start driving."

Martin sat in the back with the juice and oranges. Stan drove, while Steve sat before Martin in the front passenger seat.

"The thing is," Steve said, "our mission is to expose the alien conspiracy, but we need pictures. We came here to find Benny Jones, but we also brought our cameras. We have seen the UFOs, trust me."

"Right," Martin said, forcing a grin. He kept the gun loosely in one hand behind Steve's seat. Neither of them would be quick enough to disarm him, and he really had no intention of shooting anyone. He just wanted to be alive and get to see Chloë in Los Angeles. Anything that came between him and that goal was a distraction best avoided. Call it situational aikido.

"We believe the main alien invasion base is beneath Los Angeles," Steve said. "Makes sense, doesn't it? They have covered the ground with millions of people and houses, but underneath the city is a vast network of tunnels. In the middle of the tunnel network is a kind of queen bee hive, and in there they have a starship big enough to hold a million or more aliens."

Martin yawned. "You've seen too many movies."

"No, really," Stan said in all seriousness as he drove, and the Hummer labored up and down sand dunes.

Martin found it disconcerting to hold two circus clowns at gunpoint in the desert—but better this than the other way around.

Stan continued, "There is an underground alien rail network all around the earth. There is even a station out here in the desert. We've been in it."

"We couldn't stay in there," Steve said. "It was too hot. They had surveillance all over the place. We saw all kinds of humans, aliens, zombies, vampires, you name it."

Martin sat up. "Don't tell me—zombie mannequins work for them."

Stan looked at Martin sharply. "How did you know?"

Martin sat back, stunned. "I saw them. They tried to kill me."

Steve threw his arms up. "So what are we arguing about? Those same mannequins or zombiekins probably caught Benny out here and killed him."

"What was Benny doing?" Martin asked cautiously.

"Jumping," Steve said. "He wanted to get in quick, take pictures and video. We were going to airlift him out by chopper. He never showed up at the rendezvous."

"You okay?" Stan asked Martin.

"Shocked."

They rode in silence for a bit.

"Where's the body?" Stan asked.

Martin pointed ahead. "See that sort of squiggle in the sand? I spread his jumpsuit out so someone could easily find it."

"I hope the goons didn't see it already," Steve said.

"Where did you glide in from?" Stan asked.

"Up in the mountains. Tiny station of some kind. Jacinto City."

Stan nodded. "Goons and aliens are in on it together. They've got stations like that everywhere—not long now til they totally seize power."

"Them and the United Nations and the socialist health care freaks," Steve said. "They must be stopped."

The Hummer drew nearer to the desiccated remains of one Benny Jones, late of the Nevada something militia—Freedom Fries Brigade maybe.

Steve told Martin, "You are young, my friend. You'll realize one of these days that nothing is as it seems. Your government is the enemy."

"Praise be to Al-Balaam," Martin said in an inspired moment.

Both men ignored the peril at their backs in the form of Martin's weapons. They whirled in unison and recited, "Blessed be His Holy Name. Al-Balaam is our Savior." Each raised his right hand in a modified *Sieg Heil* salute. "He will rapture us from the aliens and the evil gummint."

Martin had a picture of clowns being lifted into clouds, with a choir of creationists humming in pious solemnity, while rays of light surrounded an indistinct savior-looking figure holding a crook and draped in a folded blanket, with his arms spread and sheep milling about. "You guys know the Reverend Damual Shultz?"

They looked terrified. "Only by name and reputation."

Martin smiled thinly. "I was visiting with him just yesterday evening. You ever been to Bombay Beach?"

They shook their heads, humbly admitting they heard much talk of it.

"You know Gramma?"

They nodded. "We know about the folks there along the beach. They been there a long, long time," Steve said. "I think some of them are a thousand years old or more."

"I believe just about anything right now," Martin said, remembering Bombay Beach in his own experience. His priorities lay in the here and now. Was there any hope still with Chloë Setreal? Only one way to find out—escape from here in one piece, and see her face to face.

"You will, brother, you will," Steve assured him.

"There it is," Stan said. He pulled the Hummer to a stop with squealing wheels. His clown hat fell off, and he put it back on with two gloved hands.

"We'll just be a few minutes," Steve said sincerely.

Martin waited while the two men climbed out and walked in a horrified posture toward their relative's bones. Benny Jones' skull grinned up at them.

Reverently, Steve gathered the bones in to the empty flight suit. Stan added more bones as he found them. Martin watched as they collected leg femurs, arms, ribs...

"It's all here," Steve said. "Thank you, brother. Thank you so much."

"Bless the Lord Al-Balaam," Martin said. He kept the pistol handy, but felt more relaxed now.

"We have it all," said Stan. He held a hand on a sobbing Steve's shoulder as the older man cradled the jumpsuit with his son-in-law's bones against his chest.

"Bless you," Stan said sincerely. A sobbing Steve sat in the front passenger seat, hunched over the bones in the flight suit. His clown face looked genuinely distressed. Stan drove while speaking. "We'll be of this goon reservation in fifteen minutes. Can we drop you off somewhere?"

"I'll let you know," Martin said.

"Here is where we begin evasive maneuvers," Stan said.

"We always dump the vehicle after we leave the reservation. They can trace it."

Stan said, "Heads up."

Martin spotted a gate of some kind about a quarter mile ahead on a road he had not noticed before. Around the gate were several buildings that had a certain gummint look to them. He could even see tiny figures milling about—security guards.

Stan took the Hummer down into a wash, really low down. They passed underneath some rusty, hanging chains and other debris.

"We're out," Steve said.

"That simple?" Martin said with astonishment.

"We're back in the real world," Stan said. "Hide the gun under the seat. We're dealing with real cops now. You can get nailed. We'll deny anything."

"Fine," Martin said. "Let's stop and fill the tank."

"Whatever you say, boss," said Stan. He found a filling station, pulled in, and used his credit card to put gasoline in the vehicle. "Now what?" he asked, rejoining Steve in the front.

Martin said, "Drive to the nearest Greyhound bus terminal."

There were no dirty tricks. Stan complied, and in ten minutes they approached the next station in Martin's journey. He said, "Oh look, there is the Greyhound bus terminal. Pull over in there."

"That's it?" Stan said.

"You'll see in a moment."

Steve exchanged looks with Stan, then looked back at Martin with a strangely conspiratorial glance out of the corners of his eyes. "Gonna turn us loose, are you?"

They pulled into a driveway of the busy terminal at the edge of Palm Springs. A group of Hare Krishnas in orange robes were chanting and beating drums, clicking little finger cymbals, dancing, and swaying about.

"You should fit right in here," Martin told the two clowns.

"Those are some of the Watchers," Stan said. "They're everywhere."

"This is one of their terminals," Steve added.

"Right. Park the car and leave the keys. No suspicious moves. I'm desperate," Martin said.

"We believe you," Steve said. "I have what I need, brother. You are on your own. Bless the Lord Al-Balaam."

"Holy be His name," Stan said as he pulled the emergency brake.

"Leave the engine running."

"Anything you say, brother."

The two men got out and walked across a driveway, to stand in a throng before the terminal. And endless series of buses pulled in and out amid plosions of diesel exhaust and engine roar. Hundreds of passengers to and from all points across Amerika milled about.

Steve held the bundle of cloth with its bones close to his chest, while Stan stood obediently beside him. Fellow travelers paid no attention to their clown suits. They looked submissive, leaving all things in Lord Al-Balaam's capable hands, and staring after the man who had led them to Ben Jones.

Martin left the gun under the back seat, along with the rifle. He pushed a bit of stray canvas over the weapons to mask them. Then he climbed into the driver's seat and strapped on the safety belt. Without any further look at the two anarchist lunatics who would have to take a bus home to Nevada in their circus costumes, Martin backed the Hummer out and found his way toward Interstate 10. He headed to Los Angeles. Things would play out according to the Lord Al-Balaam's mysterious ways.

Chapter 12. Los Aliengeles

A hot desert wind blew in Martin's hair and sandpapered his cheeks as he drove rapidly and surely toward Los Angeles. He had a full tank, enough to make it to the UCLA area in Los Angeles. Again, it would be a two hour drive or so. That's what he'd said to himself in all innocence yesterday evening. Hopefully, this time it really would just be two hours.

The rag top fluttered pleasantly in the hot desert wind. Martin almost smiled to himself, knowing he would soon be on his knees before his beloved, telling her of his adventures and explaining he was innocent of all charges. They would go out for sushi at that place with the windows and their many and varied odd reflections. You could lose yourself in a place like that. In one window you were there, in another window you weren't, in a third window you were with the love of your life hunched over lunch with chopsticks, and in a fourth window you had both vanished.

That's life.

About an hour out of LA, Martin heard faint sirens behind him. He looked in the rearview mirror and saw a Highway Patrol vehicle with flashing lights gaining on him. It was a powerful black and white cruiser that could outrun anything among the stars.

Martin let the cops get close behind him, to make sure he was who they were after.

He heard a voice on a megaphone, "Motorist in the Hummer— Pull over now."

So he changed lanes obediently and pulled over onto the shoulder.

He might have the guns to explain, but these were the police.

He didn't care now. It was out of his hands. The police cruiser pulled in behind him. Another black and white unit zoomed in on a trail of dust and sharply braked in front of him. They had him pincered.

Moments later, the doors opened in front.

The car behind stayed insular, mirror-windowed, mysterious.

Two highway patrolmen in khaki uniforms with light blue trim stepped out. They wore campaign hats and touched their sidearms to make sure of their readiness. Slowly and deliberately they walked toward the Hummer. Each wore opaque, shiny aviator-style sunglasses that masked their eyes.

Martin kept his hands on the steering wheel where they could see he would not resist.

The closer of the two said, "Good morning, Sir. Can I see your driver's license and registration?"

Martin smiled. "I'm afraid I was robbed. I have no money or I.D., and I welcome being arrested."

"Step from the car, please."

"Sure. No problem."

The cop signaled to the rear car, and they blinked their headlights on and off as a return signal. Whatever it meant, Martin no longer cared. He was worn out, finished, flat line exhausted.

The cop frisked him briefly, without really caring.

Overconfident, Martin thought.

"Anything you wish to declare?"

"The men who robbed me had weapons under the rear seat. I was able to steal their car and escape."

The cop had heard it all, and did not look surprised. At least, as much as Martin could make out from the unflinching face, the lack of expression (almost like those zombie mannequins), and the covering shades.

"Thanks for your honesty," said the one cop. "I think we can be friends."

The other was more businesslike. "Sir, the CHP will impound your vehicle and check for evidence. You are under arrest..."

What bogus crap charges are you making up?

"...For the murder of Marsha Starker in San Diego. You have the right to remain silent. Anything you say may be used against you..."

The other cop walked around the Hummer and participated in handcuffing Martin to his front.

Wind from passing cars made their uniforms flutter. Hot desert grit flurried around them.

Once again, the sun over Los Angeles in the distance, to the west, began to look like a bloody egg or eye or beating heart in a sky swirling with plasma and alien planet clouds.

"Is that too tight for you?" asked the first cop about the cuffs.

"I'll be fine," Martin said. "I did not kill anyone or do anything wrong."

"Let's go," said the passenger cop, leading Martin to the front police car. He opened the back door and shielded Martin's head with his palm as Martin compliantly climbed into the car. He sat behind the grill, feeling utterly safe for the first time in many hours.

The two policemen got in front. The driver pulled out into traffic.

The world looked so normal, and yet so foreign.

As they moved onto the freeway, the passenger-side cop lowered his sunglasses and looked at Martin. The policeman had eyes the color of steel marbles. He had no pupils or sclera, just a gleaming steel ball for each eye. No human being had ever had eyes like those.

"You should try some eye wash," Martin said. "I can recommend a brand."

"Thanks, but the sunglasses work best. Your planet has harsh underlying radiation."

They drove in silence for about ten minutes.

Then the driver said, "Bid your world goodbye. You will never see this planet again from the surface."

The other cop said, "Life underground isn't bad for you workers. We feed you well, and you get play time once a surface week. You can even mate if you wish, but we do not encouraging breeding young of your species."

The driver cop said, "It's not fair to the young. You'll be like in a zoo, but you don't want them to suffer unnecessarily. They need fresh air and light for their pathetic lives on the surface."

"Here we go," said the passenger cop.

The powerful pursuit car smoothly and purposefully treaded the eight lane freeway until, at a sweet spot lost in complexity, it drove down a ramp lit on all sides by rows of amber lights, almost pink lights.

The policemen took off their sunglasses. "This is a lot more like daylight where we come from."

"Do you miss home?" Martin asked.

The driver said: "A bit. We talk about it. We have loved ones back in the World. But this is our mission. Our life. This planet will soon be our home when your species dies off like dinosaurs and the mammoths."

The other added: "You guys do a crappy job as stewards of your world."

"It's like you have a death wish," said the driver.

"So you know our history," Martin said.

"Intimately," said the passenger cop with a businesslike smile as he folded his sunglasses away.

The car fled downward, until it joined other traffic on a multitude of ramps and freeways that looped around a vast underground city swimming in pinkish-orange light.

They took a spiraling ramp deep down into the bowels of a large building.

"Where are you taking me?"

"To the processing station. You'll be fed, clothed, and prepared for your new life."

"Doing what?"

"Laboring in the fields deep down in the earth."

The police car drew to a quiet stop. They were parked by the curb in an underground tunnel. They were alone under pink lighting amid soft shadows. It was an alien station, but could have been the underground loading docks in any earthly shopping mall. It was nicely disguised, right down to the fake oil stains on the concrete road surface—and scraps of paper trapped in phony mud flows in gutters.

"Laboring in the fields of Al-Balaam?"

The two policemen freed Martin from the rear and uncuffed him. "Stay with us, and behave. No need to shoot you unless you run or make trouble."

The passenger cop grinned proudly. "Our Lord and Savior. His Word is already sweeping your world. Before you know it, your race will submit willingly."

"You don't know the Reverend Damual Shultz and his gangsters."

"What do you mean?" said the driver cop.

"We don't surrender. We die before we give in. That's what the mammoths and the sabertooths learned."

The passenger cop looked the other, puzzled. "Such a strange species."

"Let me illumine your darkness," Martin said. With that—all in one motion—he struck the two emergency flares he took from his cowboy boots. Tearing them across the grill, he illumined the inside of the patrol car with a blinding magenta light, a magnesium hell on their gray eyes, with bluish-white stellar needle-fury in the centers of the ravenous little fires.

The two aliens cried out silently and cringed backward with their hands (or paws) over their eyes.

Martin in one smooth motion took the service automatic from one of them and shot each through the chest. They slumped on the concrete walk, bleeding greenish lizard blood or whatever that stuff was. He wiped his baseball cap, with the neo-Nazi decoration on it, in the gore so that UCLA people could analyze it later. He dragged the bodies away and dumped them in the car trunk, but first yanked off their collar cameras to use as proof later. It was the job those stupid Freedom Fries fanatics had not managed to accomplish.

He said out loud, "When you're this pissed off, anything is possible. Nobody will stop you, not even a bunch of fucking aliens."

Just as the doors were starting to open, and prison wardens came out to accept the prisoner, Martin drove away with the patrol car. It was all so fast that they would need to check the surveillance videos, if they had such things down here.

Just to be sure, he dumped the police car in an underground (way, way in the dark below) garage and started walking. The streets down here in underground Los Alienangeles were dimly lit. Thousands of buildings glowered in umber twilight, and the myriad streets and underground boulevards were thronged with all manner of odd looking people and automobiles.

Martin flagged down a taxi driven by a green-skinned man whose cheekbones bore faint, shimmering reptile scales.

"Yo bud," said the driver. "Need a lift?" He was a very light green, like spring tea. His hair color was an off-blackish, off-blueish gray. He had moss-green eyes, with square pupils on sea-green eyeballs.

"Yeah. I want to go to Uptown LA."

"Get in," said the brawny-armed driver, who wore a white muscle shirt and Elvis haircut with a shiny black curl in back. His greenness was faint enough to just be noticeable in the weak light underground, where it was always nighttime. "You want the human side?"

"Yeah."

"Sounds urgent," said the driver, trying to stay laid back while pressing down the gas. When you did this all day for a living, everything was routine.

"It's about a girl," Martin said.

"Of course. I understand. That's so universal." The driver applied g-force on the pedal. The taxi smoothly but firmly hauled off, pressing Martin back in his seat. The interior smelled of otherworldly pizza made with strange sauces and weird cheeses and unnatural sausage slices. From the vaguely familiar machine smell, Martin realized that aliens had been making fast food and packaged lunches on earth for generations. Maybe the Industrial Revolution and Thomas Crapper and other fundamental evolutions had come about through xenozoic influences.

The driver followed Martin's suggestions as best he could to find his way to a station on the intermetro. After a few wrong turns, Martin from the back seat spotted what he was looking for. He pointed. "Is that it?"

"Yup," said the driver. Ahead lay an underground metro station, looking surprisingly Parisian or New Yorkish. They drove slowly over an iron bridge studded with bolts, just like on the surface. The driver said by way of conversation, "Say, this must be a very special girl."

"She is," Martin said. "Very mysterious."

"How's that?" said Elvis, pulling close at a stained, much-used sidewalk whose gray hues were a mix of stone, grease, and human or alien sweat.

"Mysterious? Well, for one thing, her name is Chloë. That's

with these two strange little dots over the e."

The driver shrugged. "That's easy."

"Yes?" Martin eagerly pressed with both hands against the driver-passenger screen. "You know what it means?"

"It's called a diaerhesis," said the driver. "It's also known as a trema. It's over one or the other of two vowels, signaling they are to be pronounced separately. So zoölogy is zoh/ology, not *zuu*logy."

"Wow, you're smart."

"I remember it because it sounds so much like the other thing."

"You mean—?"

"Yeah, don't say it. The ride's free."

"Really?"

"Sure. You boarded in a *Grelp* Zone. Didn't you notice?"

"I thought it was the other kind of zone." Martin had no idea what the alien zones were, but the way he said it, there must be at least one other type, as a mathematical imperative.

"You're thinking of a *Xlurf* Zone. Nahh… don't worry. I wouldn't stop for you in one of these. Good luck with that girl."

"Thanks," Martin said, exiting the cab with a wave of gratitude. *Thanks for your Grelp. Xlurf's up.*

Not all aliens were as evil as one might think. *Even aliens have feelings*, he thought. He had no money or he would have tipped the guy.

However: *alieni delendi sunt*. The aliens must be destroyed. That would be the mandate of a new resistance movement he planned to join if he could find it. Or else he would help create one.

But first he must escape from Los Aliengeles.

He must go home to Chloë.

As he walked into the metro station—still in this twilit, occult underworld LA of Los Alienangeles underneath the unsuspecting human LA—Martin had a strategic hunch that the aliens had become so good at imitating humans that they had begun to fool themselves. They would be an easy target for a resistance movement. Martin was sure a resistance movement existed. For all he knew, Damual Shultz and his gangsters ran it. It was dirty work, but someone had to do it

He walked across an underground street, waiting for traffic to rush past him. He was like a rock in midstream, with a million things flowing on all sides. Nobody noticed him. He entered the station, which was filled with people (and others). It echoed with a constant stream of loudspeaker announcements drifting overhead, under decorous wrought-iron trusses from centuries gone by—mingling voices and destinations in whispering feminine-like voices, some with lizard sibilance, others with feline purring undertones. All the arrival and destination info blended in the atmosphere with a hot, rushing wind spiraling up from flying underworld trains.

Martin made his way along gloomy corridors, amber-glowing passages, steamy mezzanines, smoky squares full of bodies, to a concrete platform that would look normal in any human capital from Buenos Aires to Shanghai, from Chicago to Paris; maybe because those places had already acquired a tinge and a patina of strangeness.

People, zombies, vampires, aliens, and more creatures all mingled on the platform. Metro trains came and went. Announcers spoke in a variety of sibilant voices, from lizard to human to alien and more. Martin found the track that had all sorts of strange writing on it, but he recognized in English the words *Los Angeles Points West.* When the train rushed in on a blast of hot underground air and stopped, and the doors slid open, he joined a throng of blurry figures moving in and out of the coach. The doors slid shut, he stood holding an overhead strap along with hundreds of other strangers, and the train moved rapidly out of the station heading west into Los Angeles. Nobody stopped to ask him for his ticket. He didn't have one. It was the only illegal thing he'd done since this entire nightmare started.

Chapter 13. Chloë

In her darkened apartment, Chloë Setreal sat mourning the loss of her newly-found love. She had soared so high, only to be let down. Her roommates were off at school. Chloë was still pinned to her chair by a broken leg. She had so hoped that Martin would come to bring her sushi and love and security, which she needed and desired more than all the adoration of stupid producers in the world. She could have any man she might want, but virtually none ever appealed to her heart. What she craved were the things only Martin had offered: authentic, decent, true, sincere, romantic… she could go on counting his wonderful qualities, but now this apparent disappointment had shattered her dreams.

She had been watching television too long. She was an action girl, eager to return to work at Alienopolis and support the global superheroes campaign.

Behind shuttered windows, surrounded by comfort food, she watched the latest news. A pretty young anchor woman said, "Police in San Diego have dismissed charges of murder against a young homeless man known on the streets as Jimmy Sprocket. It was thought that he might be the young Caucasian suspect known as the Beach Killer—of brown hair, slender build, and medium-tallish height—that authorities have sought for twenty-four hours. Sprocket was seen bicycling through the dead woman's neighborhood and chatting with an unknown male at a bus stop during the rain. Subsequently, neighbors identified the dead woman as a dangerous psychopath who had escaped from the Edgemoor facility and who had been masquerading as Josie Klein, whom in reality she had murdered a week earlier. Police released Mr. Sprocket and then arrested him on charges of stealing a bicycle he was riding, which belonged to the late Josie Klein's neighbors.

The phone rang, and Chloë answered. "Yes?"

"Miss Chloë Setreal?"

"Yes, this is she." Utterly mystified, she was horrified at the next news.

"Miss Setreal, do you know a man named Martin Brown?"

"Yes?" Her voice sounded tremulous. *What now?*

"I am Detective Hanswurst of the Los Angeles Police. We have received a body in the morgue with papers identifying it as Martin

Brown. His wallet had your name and contact information, surrounded by pictures of hearts. I am so sorry, Miss Setreal."

"Oh my god," Chloë said. "Oh, Martin."

"I have to ask one more thing of you, Miss. Would you mind coming in to identify the body? I know this is a terrible ordeal for you, but the law demands closure."

"Oh, Martin," she said. "Yes," she added with a sigh. "I will do it as my duty. With a heavy heart."

"I will have a patrol unit at your address in a few minutes."

"I have a broken leg."

"We will send an ambulance at the police department's expense."

"Thank you."

When she hung up, she began to cry. So he was in Los Angeles. He had come here. Of course, he had stolen ten grand from Alienopolis Corporation's bank account, but still… somehow, she had feelings for him. And now this. It would be good closure for her.

Heavy-hearted, she waited by the door. The knock came, and two very nice EMT persons—a young man and a young woman in gray overalls, with LA County across chest and back—put her on a stretcher. They wheeled her down the stairs after locking her apartment door for her and handing her the keys. They put her in an ambulance and drove her, sobbing all the way, to a hospital. There, a priest and a rabbi met her. Together, they traveled down long, harshly lit hospital corridors where people in blue and pink and purple and white surgical scrubs came and went.

A policewoman with a diplomatic manner and pretty face met her at the morgue entrance. "How are you, Miss Setreal?"

"Call me Chloë. I've been better."

"I understand. Would you like me to hold your hand?"

"Yes, please."

The young policewoman had a firm but gentle grip. "All you have to do is look. It will be over in a minute."

"I understand." Chloë nodded and tried to stop from bursting out in a long, drawn-out wail.

They wheeled her into a tiled, awful room. There, they moved her gurney under a bright, harsh overhead light.

As the morgue attendants pulled the body from a slot in the wall, the policewoman explained, "We were able to track the man down in Westwood. He had hacked your company's bank account, using money you advanced him for his trip to Los Angeles. With the underlying data, he was able to crack the firewall and empty one of the accounts. Here he is now."

Chloë gasped as the body was unveiled. The morgue attendants, wearing white, wheeled the sheet-covered corpse close enough that she could see his face. When they pulled a white observation sheet away, Chloë's heart was ready to break. When she saw the corpse, she was flooded with a sense of relief and unreality, as if the law of gravity had been repealed.

She felt as if she were floating on air. "That is not my Martin. That is not Martin Brown. I don't know who that man is."

The policewoman was surprised, but recovered quickly. "We were wondering about that. When we cornered him, before the shoot-out, he tried to tell us he was not Martin Brown."

"Who did he say he was?" Chloë asked in shock.

"He said his name was Tony Cofoni. He said he had stolen Martin Brown's wallet and that Brown did the bank job. Now we see that he was trying to frame this Martin Brown, whoever that is."

Chloë asked through tear-streaming eyes, "So Martin didn't do it?"

The policewoman shook her head and said, "No, my dear. If this is not Martin, then your Martin is innocent as the driven snow. Where do you suppose he is?"

She said through her tears, "He kept calling and telling me he was coming to be with me. Now I believe him. Oh, Martin."

The subway from the underworld pulled through daylit, human Los Angeles. Martin stood anonymously among the other passengers, except that he was noticeable for his tawdry, ripped clothing, his gaunt features, the circles under his eyes, and a bloody gash across the bridge of his nose. His hair looked rumpled, and he might need a bath. But in the big city, nobody noticed details like that much. They just held their straps, looked the other way, and leaned apart from you in case you had a smell.

Martin stepped off the metro and began walking the remaining few blocks to the UCLA campus. There would be a long fight ahead to reclaim the world from its phantom occupiers—the alien plague that was slowly taking over.

The sun was a big bloody tomato floating amid a violent Jupiter spot of brine in a smoggy LA sky. Folks spoke of this place by various mythic names—like the City of Angels, or Lost Angeles, or the City of Aliens. Today, Martin would call it Found Angeles. It was the first step in the Resistance yet to come.

As he neared Chloë's apartment, Martin finally summoned the courage to call her one more time. This would be his last try. If she said no or hung up again, he would accept her verdict and walk away manfully, leaving her alone and never bothering her again. He would have to save the world without her—a sad and unimaginable fate, though the universe was at stake.

The phone rang in his trembling hand.

He looked and felt a mess—bloody, bedraggled, unshaven, mussy-haired, in need of a bath and new clothes. But he had made it to Chloë's address as he had vowed he would, no matter what.

The phone rang, and he heard her precious voice. "Hello?"

"Chloë, I love you more than anything in the world. Before you hang up, I just wanted you to know that you are the goddess of my heart, the love of my life, and my destination in this universe."

He paused to let her say what she would.

As he stood in the smog and bloody sunlight, surrounded by apocalyptic light and smoky fumes, she said only, "Oh, Martin" in the most loving voice. "I need you so. Come up here quickly so I can kiss you and you can hold me."

Martin whooped and ran up the stairs to knock on her door, which stood open to let him into her heart forever.

Clocktower Books – San Diego

Thank you for joining us in this breathtaking romp.

To learn about other exciting books from the authors including Rok Chilla and more, visit Clocktower Books at

https://www.clocktowerbooks.com

Author's personal website:

https://www.johntcullen.com

Read most titles half free/try-buy at Galley City:

https://www.galleycity.com

Galley City employs the bookstore model, as JTC calls it. You can sit in the bookstore and read for free all day. You just can't take the book home without paying for it. The Galley City (read-a-latte) theory is that by the time you reach halfway, you'll know whether you care enough to learn the ending and therefore buy the book. E-book prices especially are usually no more than you'd pay for a good cup of coffee or latte. While the coffee is gone in a minutes, you'll get many hours of reading pleasure for the cup of a latte. So read half free/try-buy the whole book at Galley City!

Please, tell your friends; help spread word of mouth to support the author!

Made in the USA
Monee, IL
22 February 2025

12499472R00090